About Barbara Hannay

Reading and writing have always been a big part of Barbara Hannay's life. She wrote her first short story at the age of eight for the Brownies' writer's badge. It was about a girl who's devastated when her family has to move from the city to the Australian Outback.

Since then, a love of both city and country lifestyles has been a continuing theme in Barbara's books and in her life. Although she has mostly lived in cities, now that her family has grown up and she's a full-time writer she's enjoying a country lifestyle.

Barbara and her husband live on a misty hillside in Far North Queensland's Atherton Tableland. When she's not lost in the world of her stories she's enjoying farmers' markets, gardening clubs and writing groups, or preparing for visits from family and friends.

Barbara records her country life in her blog, *Barbwired*, and her website is **www.barbarahannay.com**

Runaway Bride

Barbara Hannay

First published in Great Britain 2012
by Mills & Boon, an imprint of Harlequin (UK) Limited.
Harlequin (UK) Limited, Eton House, 18-24 Paradise Road,
Richmond, Surrey TW9 1SR

© Barbara Hannay 2012

ISBN: 978 0 263 22653 9

Harlequin (UK) policy is to use papers that are natural, renewable and recyclable products and made from wood grown in sustainable forests. The logging and manufacturing process conform to the legal environmental regulations of the country of origin.

Printed and bound in Great Britain
by CPI Antony Rowe, Chippenham, Wiltshire

Also by Barbara Hannay

Bridesmaid Says, 'I Do!'
Rancher's Twins: Mum Needed
Molly Cooper's Dream Date
A Miracle for His Secret Son
Executive: Expecting Tiny Twins
The Cattleman's Adopted Family
Expecting Miracle Twins
The Bridesmaid's Baby
Her Cattleman Boss

Did you know these are also available as eBooks?
Visit www.millsandboon.co.uk

CHAPTER ONE

THE sports car was very low, very bright and shiny. Very red. It growled to a throbbing halt right in front of Bella, and the driver killed the motor.

'Morning, Bella.' His faintly amused gaze dropped to the overnight bag at her feet. 'Going somewhere?'

Damon Cavello. Again?

Twice in one week was too much.

Damon…with the same wild, dark hair and brooding, bad-boy looks she'd fallen in love with in high school.

No, not now. I can't deal with this now.

In the last ten years, she'd seen him many times on TV, of course, in a flak jacket reporting from a war zone, or poised precariously above raging floodwaters in South America, playing the ultimate foreign correspondent.

But it was a very different matter seeing him again in the flesh, especially on *this* morning of all mornings.

Bella felt as if she'd been snap-frozen. She couldn't have smiled even if she'd wanted to, and she had to swallow before she could speak.

'Hello, Damon. I've come straight from the hotel.' Last night had been her hen night. 'I've had a call about my grandfather, Paddy.'

She nodded in the direction of the sign for the Greenacres retirement home on the stone wall behind her. Then with businesslike briskness she picked up her bag, dismissing Damon Cavello with a coolness that she hoped matched his. 'Sorry, I can't chat. It's important family business.'

About to hurry inside, she was dismayed to hear the driver's door opening.

'Hang on a minute,' Damon called as he got out.

With the flashy sports car as a backdrop, he should have looked cocky or faintly comic, but he looked neither.

Unfair. He was dressed in a faded black T-shirt and jeans, and in these clothes, with the added advantage of darkly lashed grey eyes and rumpled dark hair, he was as disturbingly sexy as ever.

'I said I can't talk, Damon. I have to go. Paddy's disappeared.'

'Take it easy, Bella. I can tell you what's happened.'

Dumbfounded, she gaped at him.

He said, 'Your grandfather has run away with my grandmother.'

A wave of dizziness threatened Bella. Her knees sagged. She *really* couldn't deal with this now.

A mere hour ago her fiancé, Kent, had left her hotel room with her diamond engagement ring in his pocket and a new lightness in his step. Minutes later, she'd received a phone call from Greenacres with the news that her grandfather had apparently disappeared.

She'd assumed the old trickster was simply playing hooky. It had happened before. Any minute now there'd be news that Paddy had been found at the bowls club, or on the banks of Willara Creek, fishing. She'd never dreamed—

'The Greenacres people rang me an hour ago and I've been checking it out,' Damon said. 'From all accounts, Paddy and Violet took off from here last night in Violet's car.'

'For heaven's sake. A joy-ride?'

'I've spoken to the fellow who runs the servo on the outskirts of town. He says they woke him up some time past midnight and begged him to fill their tank. They told him it was an emergency and they were heading north.'

'An emergency?' She frowned. 'It's not a joy-ride, then. How far north?'

'That's the burning question. They could be heading anywhere up the coast, possibly all the way to Cairns, and that's at least two days' drive. An elderly couple might take longer. The guy at the servo reckons they were on some kind of mission, and they were headed north-east, for the coast road.'

Bella rubbed at her brow as she tried to take this in. 'But—but that's crazy. They're too old to just take off like that. They're in their eighties, for goodness' sake. Paddy has a pacemaker.'

'And Violet has high blood pressure.'

At this she looked up, and without warning, her gaze locked with Damon's. For a fraught moment, she forgot everything as she reconnected with the silvery grey gorgeousness of his eyes.

So many memories…

No. *Heavens, no,* she mustn't start remembering now…

'This is ridiculous,' she snapped, deliberately shifting her gaze and letting out an audible sigh. 'It would help if we could ring them, but Paddy doesn't have a mobile phone. When he moved into Greenacres, he said everyone knew where to find him—he didn't need a mobile.'

'It was the same with Violet. Last thing she wanted was her phone going off at the hairdresser's or in church. If people wanted her, they could wait till she got home.'

'So...what can we do? Call the police?'

'I don't think there's any need to panic,' Damon said carefully. 'Actually, I've got it sorted.'

'How?'

'I'm going after them.'

'Oh.' Bella drew a deep breath, let her gaze travel over the flashy red sports car. 'In this?' She raised a critical eyebrow.

He *almost* smiled. 'Yes, Bella. In this. And yes, I know it's a bright red phallic symbol, but it was all the hire car agency in this tinpot town could offer me. And it's fine. It's a hell of a lot faster than the car our grandparents are driving.'

Damon turned to leave. Having dutifully informed her, he was clearly in a hurry to get going. 'I'm glad I saw you, but if I'm going to catch this pair I should hit the road.'

She almost called, 'Wait!' This was all happening too quickly—yet another surprise in a very surprising morning. But if she called Damon back, she wasn't sure what she would say.

As if sensing her dilemma, he looked back at her with a frown. 'How did you get here? Do you have a car?'

She shook her head. 'I came straight from the hotel.' All her friends, including her bridesmaid, Zoe, were back at the hotel sleeping off the hens' party. 'I was lucky enough to grab Willara's one and only taxi.'

'Let me give you a lift, then.' He said this politely, but without enthusiasm as if he was as cautious and tense as she was. 'Are you going back into town?'

'Actually, I should go to Blue Gums to see my father.' She had to tell her dad about Paddy's disappearance, as well as the news that she and Kent were no longer getting married. She wasn't looking forward to delivering either message.

'I can drop you off. The farm's on the way out of town.'

Bella hesitated. Getting into a sports car with Damon Cavello, her high-school sweetheart, was too much like a blast from the past.

It felt ridiculously dangerous—very Red Riding Hood and the wolf.

This man had always been the haunting *'what if?'* in her life.

But this morning his offer was also her best option. 'Thanks,' she said just a little too breathlessly.

She dropped her overnight bag next to his in the boot, and their two bags—her soft leather holdall and his scuffed, heavy-duty canvas duffle—nestled companionably together.

It was an unsettling sight.

Mad with herself for feeling nervous, she slipped into the luxurious leather passenger seat and buckled her seat belt. Damon slid behind the wheel and she caught a teasing whiff of his cologne, spicy, exotic and manly. She wondered where on the planet he'd bought it. Europe? The Middle East? Somewhere in Asia?

So not the way she wanted to be thinking.

She supposed she should think of something to talk about. She knew Damon had gone to Kent's bucks' party last night, but if she mentioned that she might find herself having to explain about their wedding cancellation. This was possibly sensible as Damon was a wedding guest, but it all felt too difficult right now. Damon would ask questions she wasn't ready to answer.

Anyway, he was about to take off up the highway. And fortunately, he wasn't in a chatty mood. He made no attempt at conversation as they drove down Willara's main street, which was quieter than ever on this early Sunday morning. Bella couldn't help wondering if he was battling similar memories to hers.

Against her better judgement, she was picturing him all those years ago as he waited for her on the street corner outside the Willara café, wearing his ripped blue jeans and ratty, faded T-shirt. She was remembering the silver spark that had lit his grey eyes whenever he saw her, and she was feeling the giddy excitement of his lips on hers, the stunning joy of his arms about her, of his lean, tough body held hard against her.

At eighteen, Damon Cavello had been raw and dangerous and addictive.

And forbidden.

He'd woken longings in her that had never been soothed.

Shut off the memories. Now. Stop it.

But as they turned right, heading out of town, the car picked up speed and Bella's sense of déjà vu grew stronger, taking her back to another time when she'd driven off in a car with Damon.

It had been a weekend towards the end of his last year of high school. They'd been driving out to the dam to join friends for a barbecue picnic. But at the turn-off, Damon had pulled off the road in the shade of paper-bark trees, and he'd just sat there, staring at the road in front of them.

'Do you want to keep going?' he'd asked.

At first, Bella hadn't understood. 'Keep going where?'

He'd grinned. 'I don't know. As far as we feel like going. Don't you ever get the urge to just take off and see what's around the corner?'

The idea had had instant appeal, but Bella's conscience had troubled her. 'The others are expecting us at the dam.'

'It would spoil the fun if we told them what we're doing. Let them guess.'

His eyes had been sparkling with excitement and a sense of adventure, and her heart had flipped, catching his enthusiasm and loving the way he continually surprised her.

Not that she would give in too easily. 'I told my parents I'd be spending the day at the dam. I can't just take off with you.'

'We'll be fine. I'll have you home in plenty of time. Come on, Bell. Let's have an adventure.' He'd smiled, his bright gaze holding hers, and of course she'd melted faster than chocolate in a microwave.

'Kiss me first while I think about it.' Bella had *loved* Damon's kisses, hadn't been able to get enough of them. Already she'd unbuckled her seat belt and was edging closer, and his lips were soft and sexy and warm.

He was the most amazing kisser. The instant their lips met, the world had become theirs. Their kiss…their mouths touching, their lips pressing, exploring, parting...

The kiss grew hotter and hotter and it took the honking of a horn from a passing truck to drag them apart.

Bella was smiling and more than a little breathless. 'Okay, you're on. Let's hit the road.'

Taking risks had been so easy.

Back then.

The memory caused a bittersweet pang to tighten like a lasso around her heart. Without warning, she was swamped by a dark wave of depression.

She told herself it was aftershock, a reaction to the snowballing weirdness of her morning. For the past few weeks she'd been focused on her wedding, on gowns and flowers and reception menus, and she'd known exactly what was happening with the rest of her life. She was going to marry her oldest friend and neighbour, Kent Rigby. She would be a farmer's wife, living on Willara Downs next door to her father's farm.

Bella had been so certain of this—okay, yes, so *resigned* to this—that she'd abandoned her career in Brisbane.

This morning, after the decision to call the wedding off, she'd felt instant relief. Now, however, the relief was fading and she was facing the blankness of her future. No job, no plans. Just a gaping black hole. She felt as if she'd been sleepwalking and had woken to find herself directionless and alone, in the middle of a vast, empty desert.

Seeing Damon again made everything worse, stirring all kinds of dangerous memories. He reminded her of all the exciting things she'd once planned for her life, none of which had eventuated.

She'd played it safe. And where had that left her?

Jobless, partnerless, with no plans and nothing to do.

Even the task of calling off the wedding had been taken on by Kent. He'd insisted on ringing their guests, and he was asking Zoe, her bridesmaid, to help with the caterers and the hire people.

Now, her grandfather was off having some crazy, reckless adventure with Violet, and Damon was chasing after him.

And Bella would be left at home feeling flat and empty, overcome by a sense of anticlimax. Or she would be dealing with endless questions and sympathetic and curious glances from every busybody in the district.

The news of the wedding cancellation would spread like a bushfire. Country towns were notorious gossip machines.

Damon turned off the main road onto the dirt track that led to her father's dilapidated farmhouse, and Bella sat up straighter, suddenly struck by a dazzlingly brilliant idea. 'I think I should go, too,' she said.

Damon frowned. 'What do you mean? Go where?'

'I should go to look for Paddy and Violet, as well as you. You can't stop in every town. I can check out the places you miss. I can get another hire car.' She pointed towards the sky. 'With a roof.'

It was the ideal diversion, exactly what she needed. Apart from her genuine concern for their grandparents, the trip offered a perfect excuse to get out of Willara for the next few days.

There was, however, a longish pause before Damon responded. 'Brilliant idea,' he said at last. 'I'm sure your fiancé won't mind in the least if you go dashing up the highway.' He sent her a strange, mirthless smile. 'As long as you're back in time to marry him on Saturday.'

Bella gulped, remembering the downside to her brilliant idea. She could no longer wriggle out of confessing the truth about the wedding to Damon. 'You're right,' she said nervously. 'Kent *won't* mind.'

'Bella, don't be an idiot. Of course he'll mind. He'll be frantic. You don't have time to chase all over Queensland. You're a bride about to be married.'

'Actually...' Deep breath. 'I'm not.'

To her dismay, Damon slammed on the brakes. They weren't at the homestead yet, but clearly this news took priority. He turned to her, trapping her in an angry silver glare. 'I'm sorry.' Now he spoke very quietly. 'You're not making sense.'

Oh, help. It shouldn't be so hard to tell Damon. He was nothing to her now. He'd been gone for ten years and in that time they'd both changed. So much. Bella couldn't begin to imagine all the things he must have seen and done since he'd left Australia. They were light-years from the high-school kids who'd fooled around together.

So why did talking to him feel so very different from talking to any of her other old schoolfriends?

'The wedding,' she began, and then to her horror a small sound like a hiccup erupted from her throat. 'It— it's not happening.'

Damon's eyes pierced her. 'What's going on, Bella?'

She gulped to swallow the huge lump in her throat. 'Kent and I decided this morning. We're not getting married.'

Several geological eras seemed to pass before Damon finally reacted. Then he rubbed at his temple as if he had a headache. 'Did you—ah—say this was a mutual decision?'

'Yes.' Bella's voice was choked. 'But if you want explanations, I'm not really in the mood to give them right now.' There was no way she could explain to this man about her and Kent's lack of sparks.

'No, of course you don't have to explain,' he said. 'I'm not asking you to.'

That was a relief. She'd been dreading his probing questions—he'd had so much practice as an investigative journalist.

Damon frowned. 'The last thing you need is this extra worry about your grandfather.' He was apparently over his shock and back to normal. 'It's lousy timing.'

'You're not wrong.' Bella forced a laugh to lighten the tension inside her. 'You'd think our elders could be more considerate.'

At this, Damon actually smiled, and Bella decided to capitalise on his good humour.

'So you can see why I'd welcome a project like trying to find Paddy.'

Almost immediately, he was shaking his head.

'I'm as personally involved as you are, Damon. I'm worried about Paddy, and…to be honest, I'd like a few days' escape from Willara. You know what the gossip in this town is like.'

'But it's such an overkill. Two cars, two lots of petrol and accommodation…' Damon's voice trailed off and he drew a sharp breath, as if he'd realised the implications of his words.

Bella had realised it, too.

It might have been unintentional, but he'd more or

less suggested that it made sense for them to travel together.

Despite the warm summer's morning, she shivered. She'd had no intention of joining Damon on a road trip. For all kinds of reasons.

'It actually makes a crazy kind of sense, doesn't it?' he said quietly.

'What does?' she asked, playing dumb.

'That we should travel together.'

Her heart leapt like a wild creature unexpectedly caught in a trap. 'In this?'

'You've seen for yourself, it's a perfectly comfortable car.'

'But I can't come with you.'

'Why not?'

His voice was cool and dispassionate, as if he didn't care one way or the other about her answer. Bella had been about to make another flustered protest, but his coolness made her feel foolish.

Why shouldn't they travel together?

From a purely practical viewpoint, it made good sense to share the costs and to take turns with the driving. On a personal level, they weren't about to start anything foolish like a fling. She'd just escaped from making a serious mistake, and she had absolutely no intention of hooking up with a new man, especially *this* man who'd hurt her once before.

Besides, Damon had changed a great deal from the seductive charmer of his youth. These days, he was the perennial nomad. He'd made an art form out of being a loner. And there was something very closed and shut off about him now.

He was looking at her with a thoughtful frown. 'I

know I can handle Violet when I find her, but, to be honest, I'm not so sure about Paddy.'

It was another valid point. They still didn't know why Paddy and Violet had taken off in such a rush, and two heads might be better than one when it came to dealing with the outcome when they eventually found their grandparents.

'I guess it does make sense to go together.' Bella sent him a nervous smile. 'But you have to admit it's a very weird situation.'

'Mad,' he agreed. 'Off the planet.'

Even so, it seemed the decision was made.

'I'll have to explain to my father. He doesn't even know the wedding's off yet.'

'Will he be okay without you? I heard he's not well.'

'He's been very ill, actually, but he's on the mend. And there are people to keep an eye on him. I—I think he'll be fine.'

Damon started the car up again and they continued on down the track, around the final bend that led to the dilapidated Blue Gums homestead with its rusted roof and peeling paint and unkempt garden.

'As you can see our place has gone downhill since Mum got sick,' she said rather unnecessarily.

'I was very sorry to hear that she died.'

Bella nodded. 'You sent me a lovely card from Dubrovnik.' His message had been heartfelt and touching and she'd cried buckets. Now, just thinking about how kind he'd been, she blinked away the sudden threat of tears. 'I'm sorry. I'd like to invite you in, but although Dad's a lot better, he's not quite up to playing host.'

'That's fine. I'll wait in the car.'

'I'll be as quick as I can.' She opened the passenger

CHAPTER TWO

DAMON was grateful for the chance to sit alone in the car while he gathered his thoughts, while he tried, desperately, to come to terms with the craziness of what had just happened.

He still couldn't quite believe he'd agreed to set out on a road trip with Bella Shaw, that he'd actually been the one who suggested they travel together.

He'd been so determined to stay clear of her. Hell.

He'd assumed that he'd grown wiser in the past few years. He'd seen so much—had witnessed terrible atrocities and disasters. He'd been detained at gunpoint more times than he cared to count.

And yet…here in the town where he'd spent his five years of high school…this sleepy little town set in the middle of golden wheat fields and dusty cow paddocks…he'd stumbled on an entirely new set of dangers. Unexpected traps.

Emotional traps…in the form of his sweet, elderly grandmother, Violet, the only member of his family who communicated with him regularly, and the one person in the world he loved unequivocally.

And Bella Shaw…

Bella...of the pale silky hair, wide green eyes and lissom, almost waiflike body.

Letting out a heavy sigh, Damon propped his elbow on the car's door frame and massaged his aching forehead. He willed himself to relax, to absorb the stillness of the countryside, the muffled buzzing of insects and the distant call of a magpie.

He'd spent the past decade in voluntary exile, first as a journalist in Singapore, then Hong Kong, and in more recent years, as a foreign correspondent. He'd been busy, constantly learning, dealing with danger on a daily basis, and he could have sworn that Bella Shaw no longer had a hold on him. She'd been his high-school crush, for heaven's sake. Nothing more.

He'd liaised with many women since he left this town. Beautiful women. Wise, wicked and worldly women. And he'd found something to admire in all of them.

These days, he was a totally different person from the boy who'd lived here. In high school he'd still been impressionable, trying for the most part to fit in with the local kids, despite the wars at home.

Since then, he'd discovered his true calling as a loner, an observer always on the fringes, never staying in one place for too long. A man with no ties. A man who was no longer brought to his knees by the merest fleeting smile from one particular girl.

He had been so sure it was safe to come back.

It should have been easy. Dead easy. Bella was marrying Kent Rigby.

Those fateful words: 'I do!' A gold band on her finger. In one short ceremony Damon could close the door on his past, could free himself of haunting memories. Forever.

What irony.

Instead of burying his past, he'd dragged it with both hands into his present. Bella was still single, and he was going to be in constant contact with her, up close and personal, for an indefinite period.

Damn. Shoving the car door open, Damon jumped out. Hands plunged deep in his pockets, he paced along the narrow dirt track beside the Blue Gums fence line while the shock of the wedding cancellation reverberated through him like a string of explosives.

What had gone wrong with their wedding plans?

There'd been no sign of a problem at the bucks' party last night.

Thud.

The bucks' party. He felt a slam of guilt like a fist in the guts. He'd been such a jerk, made a damn fool of himself. He'd fronted up to Kent, intending to congratulate the lucky groom, then he'd lost the plot and more or less questioned Kent's right to marry Bella.

Remembering it now, Damon groaned so loudly he frightened a flock of finches in a nearby tree. What the *hell* had he been thinking?

He couldn't blame the drink—that had come later when he'd realised how very unsmart he'd been.

Talk about uncalled for. He hadn't seen either Kent or Bella in over a decade, and he'd severely stuffed his chances with her back then. He had no right to question Kent.

And yet he'd been unable to quash his doubts. He'd told himself the doubts were crazy. Unreasonable. Kent was a great bloke, an old mate. There could be no doubt that he and Bella were destined as Willara's golden couple.

Just the same...

Damon couldn't get his head around the idea. He couldn't see how Bella would be happy as a farmer's wife, couldn't forget the way she used to joke about it.

'Shoot me now,' she used to say if anyone suggested she might live in Willara for the rest of her life.

Last night he'd spoken out of turn. This morning, it seemed his doubts had been spot on and he couldn't deny a glimmer of smug male satisfaction that he was right.

But hell, look where it had landed him.

'Damon!'

Bella's voice brought him whirling round. She was standing at the front gate, holding a small bag that probably held spare clothes. She was ready to jump in a car with him, again, although not quite in the same spontaneous way she had all those years ago...

She was wiser now, thank heavens. Wiser and warier. And so was he.

'Ready when you are,' she called.

His stomach tightened.

Bella had deliberately changed into her plainest clothes—old and slightly baggy jeans, a sensible, sunsmart, long-sleeved cotton shirt and sneakers. No makeup, just sunscreen and lip gloss.

Her hair was pulled into a tight ponytail and shoved inside a peaked cap. Sunglasses finished the picture and she hoped the message was clear: she was a flirtation-free zone.

The embarrassing thing was—it was she who needed

to remember this. Not Damon. She knew there was absolutely no risk that he'd start flirting with her. His focus was solely on finding their grandparents.

'How's your father?' he asked when he reached her.

'Not too bad, thanks.'

'He coped with the news?'

'About the wedding? Yes.'

Actually, her dad had taken the news surprisingly well. He'd talked about sparks and chemistry, the kind of fire that had, apparently, kindled his happy marriage to her mum. Bella wondered if he'd guessed that a lack of these sparks had been at the heart of her problem with Kent.

'He assures me he's fine now,' she said. 'He's only mildly concerned about Paddy, but he thinks it's great that we're going to find them and keep an eye on them. Oh, and he's hoping to see you when we get back.'

'Right,' Damon said with the grim reserve that seemed to have become his default demeanour. 'Let's hit the road.'

The sun had climbed high and Bella turned up the collar of her shirt to protect her neck.

'Are you worried about the sun?' Damon was blessed with a natural tan, thanks to Italian heritage on his father's side. He frowned at her. 'We don't have to have the top down.'

'I'm okay for now, thanks.' Risk of sunburn was not Bella's first concern today. She was worn out after weeks of tension over the wedding and she welcomed a dose of sunshine and fresh air to blow away the cobwebs.

'I'm planning to head across the downs to the coast via Kingaroy.' Damon dropped a folded map into a pocket on the inside of his door. 'I don't expect we'll need this, but I thought I'd play it safe.'

'That's not like you.'

He regarded her with a steady, cool gaze. 'I guess I've changed.' After a beat, 'Haven't you?'

'Yes, of course.' In recent years playing it safe had become a habit. So much so that her life had come to a grinding halt.

But she would worry about reinventing herself once they'd found Paddy and Violet.

'I brought a photograph of them.' She reached into her bag. 'It was taken at Greenacres last Christmas. I'm afraid we were all wearing silly paper hats, but you can see our faces quite well.'

'Brilliant.' Damon's eyes warmed as he looked at the snap of the happy trio linked arm in arm in front of a Christmas tree. 'It won't be easy to ask nosy questions without arousing suspicions, but at least this photo proves that you actually know Paddy and Violet. Good thinking.'

Bella was ridiculously pleased by this small spoonful of praise. For heaven's sake, she had to calm down. Unnerved, she looked away.

Damon was calm and businesslike. 'I think we're good to go. The Greenacres people have our numbers, so they'll ring us if there's any fresh news.' And then he started the car.

Almost against her will, Bella found herself watching him. His hands had always been strong and capable and she used to love watching him do ordinary things—anything really—catching a ball, wielding a penknife, changing gears...

The car's engine purred, she took a deep breath

and they moved smoothly forward. Within moments, fields of crops and clumps of bushland flashed past and she turned her attention to the scenery, determined that by the end of this trip she would be an expert on Queensland's geography. Not the driver.

From the start, Damon tried his best to concentrate on the road ahead and to remain impartial to Bella's presence beside him.

But she was constantly there in his peripheral vision, and he couldn't help being aware of her hands, restless in her lap, pale and delicate and city-girl cared for. Her nails were painted silver and every now and then she fiddled with her ring finger, rubbing at the skin where her engagement ring had been.

What was she thinking?

He couldn't deny he was curious about her mood now that the wedding was off. Was she heartbroken? Relieved? He couldn't tell.

It was none of his business, of course. He had to get his mind out of that groove. He should try to think of something to talk about, but the only thing they had in common were memories and they were as dangerous to negotiate as a minefield.

'So how's your father?' Bella asked him suddenly.

Damon almost groaned aloud. From his point of view, she couldn't have chosen a worse conversation opener.

One look at his face and she must have guessed this. Carefully, she asked, 'Is he still being difficult?'

'No.' Damon glared through the windscreen to the road ahead. 'We just stay well clear of each other.'

He knew that Bella would be recalling the escalating

wars he'd had with his policeman dad during the five years he'd been stationed in Willara. The final show-down had led to the cancellation of his eighteenth birth-day party, and the end of their high-school romance.

'You've certainly made sure you stayed far enough away,' she said.

Damon bristled. Talking about his father was guar-anteed to make him snappy. 'I didn't leave Australia simply to escape.'

'Didn't you?'

There was no mistaking the faint criticism in her voice. But Damon wasn't prepared to admit she was close to the truth, that reporting about other people's problems had helped him to avoid his own.

'I wanted to see the world,' he said. 'You know—broaden my mind—experience as many different cul-tures and perspectives as I could.'

'That does sound very appealing.'

There was a wistful quality to her voice. He turned to catch her expression, but her face was mostly hidden by the brim of her cap and her sunglasses.

He thought how different her past decade had been from his. While he'd been the prodigal son, she'd been the good and dutiful daughter, staying in Queensland and worrying about her parents and their illnesses. Coping with her mother's death. She'd been very close to her mother.

To make amends for his terseness, he said, 'This probably sounds clumsy, but I really liked your mother. She was terrific.'

Bella shook her head. 'That's not clumsy. It's nice. I don't get to hear it very often. Most people avoid talking about Mum. I suppose they're worried they'll upset me.' She turned to him. 'Mum liked you, Damon.'

'Until I blotted my copybook.'

'No. I know it didn't seem like it at the time, but my mother was a true-blue fan of yours.' She looked down and rubbed at her finger again. 'Did you know she'd made you a birthday cake?'

'For my eighteenth?'

'Yes, for the party that never happened.' Almost immediately, Bella groaned. 'Sorry. Forget I mentioned that.'

'Mentioned what?'

She looked momentarily puzzled, and then she smiled. Damon smiled, too, and for a heartbeat, it was dangerously almost like old times.

They stopped for a late lunch at a roadside café. Bella wasn't particularly hungry and only ate half of her toasted sandwiches, but Damon tucked into his hamburger.

On the road again, she felt her eyelids beginning to droop. She'd had very little sleep the night before. She'd tossed and turned after she'd received a late text message from Kent saying that he needed to talk. And then this morning he'd knocked on her hotel-room door at the crack of dawn, and, although she was happy with the outcome, reaching their final decision had been an emotionally draining process.

She yawned loudly.

'Feel free to sleep,' Damon told her.

'Oh, it's too early. If I sleep now, I'll never sleep tonight. I think I need to keep talking.'

'What about?'

'I don't know.' She was too tired for anything serious like politics or current affairs. Problem was, Damon had been her first boyfriend and her head was full of memories of his kisses and caresses, of the exciting journey of sexual discovery that they'd begun together.

'You could tell me about your girlfriends.'

'Not much to report there.'

'Rubbish. I've read all about you in a celebrity magazine. You've had girlfriends galore.'

She watched him silently, waiting for him to respond.

Instead, he bounced the question back at her. 'And I suppose you've had lots of boyfriends?'

Ouch. She had no intention of telling Damon Cavello about her sadly minimalist relationship history. She sighed, knowing there was one topic she should probably broach. 'I suppose I *should* explain about Kent,' she said. 'And why we decided not to get married.'

His hands tensed on the steering wheel. 'Only if you want to.'

'It's okay. I think I'd like to explain. After all, you're Kent's friend. But it's actually a rather long story.'

'We have plenty of time.'

'Yes.' She drew a deep, steadying breath. 'Well...it started when my father got really sick.'

'You've had a rough trot, Bella.'

She nodded. 'After Mum died, we were all rather lost...Dad, Paddy and I. But your grandmother was wonderful for Paddy. She went out of her way to cheer him up.'

Damon smiled. 'She has a talent for cheering people up. I'm glad she was able to help. She mentioned that your father was very low.'

'He was. He started drinking too much. Drowning his sorrows. It was really awful, actually.'

'You were away, working in Brisbane, weren't you?'

'Yes, and I didn't realise how quickly Dad was going downhill. He was neglecting the farm. He wasn't paying bills. When I realised how bad things were, I started coming home on weekends, and Kent helped out on the farm. Mending fences. Ploughing. Kent was fabulous, actually.'

Damon slanted her a piercing glance. 'Is that when the two of you became close?'

'Yes.' She looked away, then said carefully, 'I'm not sure if you ever knew, but Kent's always looked up to my father. You probably heard that Dad saved Kent from drowning when he was a kid?'

Damon nodded.

'Kent felt that he owed him a huge debt. He became very worried when Dad started the heavy drinking. Then Dad developed heart failure. He'd been literally drinking himself to death.'

'And Kent wanted to help.'

'Yes.'

'By marrying you?'

The fierce intensity in Damon's voice made her shiver. 'More or less.' She rubbed at her arms. 'Kent suggested we should get engaged, and suddenly it seemed to be the answer to all my problems. He and I would be living next door to Dad. We could keep an eye on him, get him to A A meetings and help him to run the farm.'

'And there'd be grandchildren for your father to dote on. A reason for him to go on living.'

Bella drew a sharp breath. 'That was what we hoped.'

After a beat, Damon said, smoothly, 'It sounds like a great plan. Dare I ask what went wrong?'

Oh, help. This was the hard part.

There was no way she could explain to this man who set her heart spinning at fifty paces about their lack of chemistry. 'We—ah—realised that gratitude isn't a good basis for a happy marriage,' she said quietly.

Damon's clever grey eyes narrowed. 'And it was an amicable decision?'

'Of course.'

But suddenly she'd had enough. She'd told Damon far more than she'd intended and she didn't want this clever reporter probing too deeply. 'This isn't an interview, Damon. If you don't mind, I'm done with answering questions.'

With that, she yawned dramatically and closed her eyes.

Damon drove on, and it wasn't too long before Bella's head slipped sideways. Her cap fell off revealing the soft, pale gleam of her hair. A strand escaped and fluttered gently like a golden streamer. As her head tipped farther he caught sight of the thick fringe of her eyelashes behind her sunglasses. Yes, she was definitely asleep, and he was flooded by a surge of protectiveness.

He thought about the story she'd just told him. There'd been no sign of self-pity in her voice, but he'd found her tale incredibly sad. Bella, the fun-loving, sexy and adventurous girl he'd known, had been loaded with too many responsibilities and worries.

Reading between the lines…these worries were the reason she'd been prepared to sacrifice herself in a passionless marriage. The thought of Bella trapped by duty enraged him.

But…damn it. This was so not the way he wanted to

feel. An emotional reconnection with Bella Shaw was definitely not part of his plan.

He forced his focus to the blue bitumen road stretching ahead, and to the wider, lighter blue of the sky arching above. Purposefully, he inhaled the scents of dry earth and the eucalyptus wafting in on the fresh, clean air.

For him, the allure of an open road had always been strong, and if he weren't so concerned now about Violet and Paddy he would have absolutely loved this journey. Each bend in the road was a new possibility, a chance for adventure. He was always at his happiest when he was travelling with no clear destination.

At heart, he'd never changed. He was a gypsy, a nomad.

And he was quite sure that, for a nomad like him, it had been a mistake to come home.

CHAPTER THREE

WHEN Bella woke she was aware of a strange blue-grey
light outside. She saw stands of tall pine trees flashing past. And she saw the back of Damon's dark head.

The *back* of his head? That didn't seem right. She
blinked and tried to sit up, but she was held down by
her seat belt. Her neck was stiff and she realised that
her seat had been lowered into the reclining position.
And the car had a roof.

When had that happened? She couldn't remember.

Beneath her cheek, there was something soft and
pillowy—a man's sweater with a faint hint of Damon's
exotic cologne had been rolled up to cushion her head.

She yanked on the lever that raised her seat. 'What
time is it?'

Damon smiled. 'Hey, there.'

Yawning, she reached for her water bottle and took a
few sips. That was better. 'What's the time?' she asked
again. 'Have I been asleep long?'

'It's almost five.' He pointed to the clock on the dash-
board.

'Wow. I've been asleep for a couple of hours, then.'

'More than a couple.'

Sleepily, Bella took another look at their surroundings. There was something about the light that didn't seem right for five o'clock in the afternoon. It should have been all golden and coppery and sloping in low from the west. She shivered and frowned as a terrible thought struck. 'Damon, it's not five o'clock in the morning, is it?'

'It certainly is.'

'No! It can't be.' Shocked, she sat up straighter, and pulled her jacket more closely around her. Wait a minute. Where had her jacket come from? She turned to Damon. 'Did you get this jacket out of my bag?'

'You were getting goose bumps on your arms.'

She rubbed at the stiff spot on her neck. 'But I can't have been asleep all night.'

'You were exhausted, Bella, and you needed to sleep. You've had a huge twenty-four hours.'

'I know. But don't tell me you've been driving all night?'

'I felt fine.'

'Damon, you shouldn't have. You should have stopped.'

She was beginning to feel quite angry. Guilty, too. They were supposed to share the driving. 'Why didn't you tell me you weren't planning to stop?'

'It wasn't planned. It just seemed like a good idea to let you sleep and push on.'

'But we could have stayed in a motel.'

He cocked a questioning eyebrow. 'Were you anxious to spend the night in a motel?'

'In separate rooms, of course.'

'Of course.' Faint amusement shimmered in his eyes.

Bella could feel her anger rising to the boil. 'Anyone with any sense knows you have to have adequate rest on a long road trip.' She should have guessed something like this might happen. Damon Cavello had always been a risk taker.

They rounded a curve and she shot an angry glance at the view of vast plains stretching ahead, soft in the morning light, and dotted with grazing cattle. 'So, where are we?'

'Just south of Rockhampton.'

'Rockhampton? That's ridiculous, Damon. What's the point of haring up the highway when we don't know for sure where Violet and Paddy are? We could have passed them in the night back in Gympie, or Hervey Bay.'

'I take it you're not a morning person,' he said smoothly.

She narrowed her eyes at him. Okay, she *was* being snappy, but she was justified. Damon might think he was bullet proof, but they were supposed to be a team and he should have at least consulted her before deciding to drive all night.

'I'm fine once I've had coffee.'

'There should be a coffee shop coming up very soon.'

'I still think I was making a valid point. Let me remind you, you're not still in a war zone, Mr Cavello.'

'I had noticed.'

'That means we don't need to take the risks you're so fond of. I don't fancy finding myself wrapped around a gum tree because you chose to drive all night.'

'I was fine, Bella.'

'That's not the point. From now on, we make joint decisions. If we need to drive all night, I'll be part of the decision making. I'm not just here for the ride, you know. I'll do my share of the driving.'

'I hear you.'

Annoyed by his quiet, smug responses, Bella threw in her trump card. 'And. As I said, it's crazy to race pell-mell up the highway when we don't know where our grandparents are. We're supposed to be stopping along the way and making enquiries.'

'The circumstances have changed.'

Gobsmacked, she stared at him. 'How?'

'Brenda Holmes rang from Greenacres. They've found a note from Violet.'

Bella's jaw sagged. 'You mean I slept through a phone call?'

'Snored your head off.'

If he weren't driving she would have hit him. 'When were you going to tell me?'

'When I could get a word in edgeways.'

The nerve of him to treat her like a sleeping child and then throw joking insults. Bella was sorely tempted to continue her lecture. But she supposed it would be water off a duck's back. The man was a law unto himself. Already, she was beginning to regret her rash impulse to join him on this wild chase.

'So where was this note?' she asked primly. 'And why did Brenda Holmes take so long to find it?'

'It was stuck, or caught, under Violet's neighbour's doormat. Violet must have slipped it under the door in the middle of the night. She was probably fumbling around in the dark, and it went under the mat, as well. At any rate no one saw it till last night.'

'And what did it say?'

'Not as much as we might have hoped. But it seems there's been some kind of emergency in Port Douglas, and Paddy was determined that he had to be there straight away. Violet lent him her car and apparently decided she couldn't let him travel all that way on his own.'

Bella blinked as she assimilated this news. 'But they might have driven to Brisbane and caught a plane.'

'I doubt it. The driver at the servo was certain they were definitely heading north.'

'That's true, and I've just remembered that Paddy's not supposed to fly. It's something to do with his heart.'

She let out her breath with a whoosh. She hadn't dreamed their grandparents were on some kind of mercy dash. It was such a long way for an elderly couple to drive. 'Port Douglas is even farther north than Cairns.'

'Exactly. That's why I decided to keep going.'

'I wonder what the emergency is.' She was thinking aloud now, trying to remember if Paddy had talked about Port Douglas. She had a vague feeling he *had* mentioned it.

'I think one of Paddy's mates lives in Port Douglas. I remember Paddy talking about a fellow veteran from the Korean War.'

'Can you remember his name?'

'No.' She sighed. 'It might come to me, but I'm drawing blanks at the moment. Dad might know. I'll call him later.'

At least she was feeling wide awake now. 'You should let me drive, Damon. You must be worn out.'

'We'll have breakfast in Rockhampton and then you can take over.' He shot her a wink. 'Once you've had your coffee.'

At the thought of coffee and food her stomach growled. She'd barely touched her lunch yesterday and she hadn't eaten dinner. 'I'm starving.'

'That's a good sign.'

His smile was a glimpse of the old Damon. It was the smile she'd fallen in love with.

There weren't too many eating places open at such an early hour, but they found a roadside café, popular with truckies, where a heavenly smell of coffee greeted them as soon as they pushed open the heavy glass door.

Once they'd placed their orders, Bella went to the bathroom and washed her face, freed her hair from its ponytail and gave it a good brushing. Foolishly, she wished she could leave it down. She felt more attractive and feminine with her hair bouncing about her shoulders.

You're a flirtation-free zone.

She thought about the way Damon had smiled at her a few minutes ago. There'd been a silver spark of emotion in his grey eyes. And a warmth that had sent tiny thrills rippling all the way from her head to her toes. Once again, she'd found herself thinking about their past, remembering their kisses and the exact feel of his lips touching hers and the way she used to melt.

Stop it.

Hastily, she pulled her hair back beneath the tight elastic band and jammed on her cap. She should be remembering that Damon was trouble. Back in high school, her parents had forbidden her to see him again, and they'd been wise. Soon after, he'd left town and broken her heart.

That was what she should be remembering. She was glad she had that sorted before she returned to their table.

Coffee arrived, hot and delicious, and soon after that

a massive plate of bacon and scrambled eggs with slices of hot buttered toast. Normally, Bella would be daunted by such a huge meal. This morning she was ravenous and tucked in hungrily.

So did Damon. In fact they were both so hungry, they barely talked.

But with food inside her, Bella felt more relaxed. As she buttered a second slice of toast she said, 'I guess you've eaten a lot of interesting breakfasts in different parts of the world.'

'Yeah.' He smiled. 'Like rancid meat and yak's milk in Mongolia.'

'Eeeeuuuwwww. I'm afraid I'd have to stay with less adventurous food like fried rice or crêpes.'

'There've been plenty of those.' Damon set down his coffee cup. 'You'd probably love churros and hot chocolate.'

'That does sound yummy. Where can you eat it for breakfast?'

'In Spain.'

Bella pictured Damon in Spain, walking down an old cobbled street where pretty señoritas flashed their dark eyes at him. 'Do you miss Aussie food?' she asked quickly.

He laughed and shook his head. 'Violet sends me food packages all the time.'

'Good old Violet. I'm so relieved we know where they're heading now, and we don't have to stop and search along the way.'

'It's a relief to know they haven't gone crazy,' Damon said quietly.

'Were you worried about that, too?'

'I was when I first heard that Vi was missing. It

crossed my mind that this might have been the beginnings of dementia.'

'But Paddy and Violet wouldn't both get it at the same time.'

'No, and Violet's mind's still razor sharp. She's managed to keep in regular contact with me even though I'm always on the move. And the other day, she hammered me at a complicated word game.'

This time when Damon smiled, Bella had to look away. They still had a long drive ahead, up the Queensland coast, and she'd be a mess if she kept reacting to him like this.

At least she was confident now that they'd find their grandparents, and everything would be resolved in another day or two.

Then, Damon could look after Violet, and with a little luck Bella would coax Paddy into taking a train trip from Cairns to Brisbane and she'd have him safely back in Willara in no time. Then she'd be free.

Free of marriage plans, free of old boyfriends and hopefully free of family worries. She could work out, then, what she wanted to do with the rest of her life.

She wished she felt happier about that. If only she felt free, rather than completely blank, like a deleted page on a computer screen.

Right now, she felt more lost than free.

But heavens…she couldn't start worrying about her future just yet. For now, she had to try to relax.

As they left the café, Bella was surprised by how much better she felt. She'd had a good night's sleep, her stomach was full and caffeine was pumping through her veins. She wasn't even daunted by the sight of their red sports car looking ridiculously small and low as it hunkered between the massive haulage trains in the parking lot.

'Let's have the top down this morning,' she said in a burst of enthusiasm. 'Or would you like to leave it up while you sleep?'

'Down's fine.' Damon was already pushing the appropriate lever.

Bella settled herself behind the wheel, adjusting the seat and the rear-vision mirror. She turned the ignition and the engine purred with the low throaty growl of a jungle cat.

Cool. Excitement pinged. For the first time in ages, she was looking forward to this adventure.

As they left Rockhampton behind them and headed north along the highway, the morning air was fresh and the sun not yet hot. This was cattle country, smooth and flat, with straight roads and few trees and plenty of visibility. The sky was clear and pale and endless, and a flock of galahs fluttered overhead, their rosy pink breasts a bright contrast to the soft pale grey of their wings.

Bella felt her spirits lift even higher. She put her foot down and the little car leapt in response. This was fun.

'You should try to catch some sleep,' she told Damon, but to her annoyance his eyes remained stubbornly open. Didn't he trust her driving? She pressed the accelerator a little harder, but reluctantly had to ease back when the car shot over the speed limit.

Out of the corner of her eye she caught Damon's smile. No doubt he was amused and she wished he would go to sleep.

In a bid to ignore him, she let her thoughts turn to Kent. She'd fallen asleep last night without ringing to see how he was faring with the aftermath of their break up and it had been too early to ring this morning.

She hoped Kent was okay. At least she knew he wasn't nursing a broken heart. She felt a bit guilty that she'd escaped the unpleasant job of ringing the wedding guests and the caterers, but he'd insisted that she leave him with the task.

This morning, she was truly relieved that they'd come to their senses in time. In fact, she could now look on her close brush with a serious, life-changing mistake as a useful warning. She would think very carefully before she leapt into any new relationship. She was certainly mega cautious about the man currently sitting beside her.

It was good to have these thoughts sorted, good to recognise that she felt more at peace with herself than she had in weeks.

To her relief, Damon was starting to relax, too. He stretched his legs out as far as the car's cramped interior would allow, let his head fall back and closed his eyes.

Great. Finally, he trusted her driving, and she felt better than ever.

Bella drew a deep lungful of the fresh air rushing past them. She'd never been this far north before. She took in details of her surroundings and pondered on the lives of the people living in the vast cattle stations that stretched for miles on either side of the highway.

She felt so relieved and light-hearted she might have broken into song if Damon hadn't been dozing. Instead, she hummed softly under her breath, and she was still humming when she saw the blue-and-white car appear in her rear-vision mirror.

Was that a police car?

Uneasiness lifted the hairs on the back of her neck. Hastily she checked the speedometer. *Whoops*—just over.

With a guilty grimace, she applied the brakes and hoped she wasn't in range of the police radar.

She was out of luck. Almost immediately, blue-and-red lights began to flash behind her. Damn.

The police car drew closer, the lights flashing bossily. Bella groaned, 'Oh, God,' and unhappily pulled over to the edge of the highway.

Beside her, Damon stirred. 'What's up? What's happening?'

'Police,' she muttered miserably. Wasn't this the story of her life? Every time she tried the tiniest adventure, fate slapped her down.

Damon shot a glance behind and saw the police car pulling up. 'Were you speeding?'

'Not really.'

Bella half expected Damon to swear, but he merely let out a soft, resigned sigh. She felt sick as she heard the crunch of a heavy tread on the bitumen behind them. In the car's side mirror she saw a tall, blue-uniformed figure. She sat up straight, lifted her chin to a dignified angle.

The policeman was young and puffed with self-importance. 'Good morning,' he said in an annoyingly pseudo-friendly voice.

'Morning, constable,' Damon answered.

The young policeman ignored his greeting and fixed cool blue eyes on Bella.

She tried to look innocent. 'I wasn't speeding, was I?'

The policeman shrugged. 'Can I see your licence, madam?'

'Oh? Oh, yes. Sure. It's in my bag.'

Her bag was at Damon's feet and their hands collided as they both reached for it. Their gazes met and Damon's eyes held a silent message of empathy. Then he smiled and winked.

His smile helped, but Bella was flushed and shaking as she handed over her licence. The young policeman frowned officiously and began to jot down her details in his notebook.

Beside her, Damon let out an annoyed huff. 'How about an explanation, officer? What's the problem?'

'I'll need your licence too, sir.'

Bella was sure Damon would protest this time. After all, he was merely a passenger. To her surprise he said quietly, 'Yeah. Whatever.' Then pulled his licence from his wallet and handed it over.

Now she was seriously scared. Why did the policemen want Damon's licence, as well? This couldn't be a mere speeding infringement.

Memories of Damon's reckless reputation flashed through her thoughts. He'd been pretty wild in his teens. He'd even been arrested by his own father when he was eighteen and it had caused a scandal that fired up Willara's gossips for months. Bella's parents had listened, and they'd refused to let her see him. Not long after that Damon had left town.

She'd always believed the infamous event was a storm in a teacup, blown out of proportion by small-town rumours, but she had no idea what Damon had done since then. She wasn't intimate with the details of his past ten years.

The policeman certainly seemed suspicious. Directing a mean, narrow-eyed glare at her, he reached in and snatched the keys from the ignition.

'Hang on.' Damon looked at the policeman in surprise. 'You owe us an explanation, mate. What's your problem?'

'You're the ones with the problem.' The constable spoke with annoying, self-righteous confidence. 'I'd like you both to step out of the car. This is a stolen vehicle.'

'Stolen?' Bella cried. 'That's impossible. It's a hire car.'

She felt Damon's hand close over hers, squeezing her fingers gently but firmly. 'Just do what he says,' he murmured softly. 'I'm sure we can sort this out.'

The policeman nodded. 'You'll have to come back to the station with me.'

Bella choked on a gasp. This couldn't be happening. It was a nightmare. She couldn't breathe.

But she was also as angry as she was scared. She hated the policeman's tone. Chin high, she challenged him. 'Can't we just follow you?'

'No, Miss Shaw. I'll arrange a tow truck for this car.'

'Surely you're not arresting us?' asked Damon.

The young policemen almost smiled. 'If you like, I can arrest you right here on suspicion, or you can come to the station to answer some questions.'

No! This couldn't be happening!

Horrified, Bella turned to Damon. His lovely grey eyes were dark with sympathy and a deeper, unreadable emotion. She expected him to say something, to do something, to become the risk-taking hero she knew he could be. But he simply gave an almost imperceptible shake of his head and then an equally faint shrug.

To her dismay, she knew exactly what he was telling her.

We have no choice. Come on. Let's cooperate.

CHAPTER FOUR

TRAVELLING down the highway in the back of the police car, Damon was only concerned about Bella. She sat very stiffly with her back straight, her hands tight fists in her lap. Her green eyes were fixed dead ahead, not meeting his, and he knew she was terrified and bewildered. It was more than possible she was also wondering if he really had stolen the car.

He wished he could reassure her, but it wasn't worth trying to talk within the copper's hearing. This was probably Bella's first encounter with the police, whereas he'd been pulled up more times than he cared to remember.

On many of those occasions the police had been nasty or they'd been agents of really nasty regimes, often armed to the teeth with semi-automatic weapons. Too often, they'd looked as if they wanted to shoot him, to take him off somewhere to interview him with electrodes attached.

Damon had learned fast and he knew there was always a system, always someone higher who would make the final call. The trick in these situations was patience. It wasn't worth provoking or shouting about rights. It was best to hold your tongue, stay firm and confident. Not lose the plot.

He wished he could reassure Bella that on the scale of things Australia was the best place in the world to be riding in the back of a police car. She looked so serious and white-faced, so angry and afraid.

This was beyond awful.

Bella had never been inside a police car and she was fighting a rising tide of panic. She couldn't breathe, couldn't think. None of this felt real. It couldn't be happening, and yet the tiny part of her brain that was still functioning told her this was about as real as it got.

She wished she knew what Damon was thinking. His dark face looked unbelievably calm, and she wanted to believe he was innocent. Now, when the chips were down, she felt her old loyalty to him rushing back. She didn't want to doubt him, but how could she be sure?

Problem was, she didn't really know him anymore. Had she ever really known him? There'd always been a secretive, dark side to Damon, and yet she'd jumped into a car with him yesterday as recklessly as she had when she was seventeen.

Hot tears threatened and she closed her eyes to hold them back. One thing was absolutely certain: she mustn't cry. She had to look on this nightmare as a test of her character. She had to be strong.

With her eyes closed, she let her mind escape to happier times with Damon, to the very start of those brief, sweet months when he'd been her high-school sweetheart.

It had all been very Romeo and Juliet. Very intense and poignant. And quite innocent for the most part.

Their friendship and romance had started without fanfare and in a very ordinary way on the sporting field after school.

Bella had stayed back for netball practice, and on those afternoons she couldn't take the school bus back to the farm, so she usually walked across the playing field, taking the shortcut to her grandparents' place.

Remembering it now, she couldn't help smiling.

Damon had been alone, kicking a football around. She could still picture him in his baggy striped jersey and shorts, jogging backwards with eyes fixed on a ball that he'd kicked high. He'd almost backed into her, but she'd ducked out of his way so they didn't collide. Her sudden appearance had distracted him, however, and he'd missed catching the ball.

He hadn't seemed to mind.

Bella would never forget that moment when they'd looked into each other's eyes and smiled. Damon was so incredibly hot, with his wild dark hair and sexy, square jaw and wonderfully broad shoulders. She could still recall the flash of silver in his grey eyes. And right from the start there'd been a thrilling air of danger about him.

Amazingly, Bella hadn't been scared. When Damon smiled at her she felt no fear at all, just a fierce rush of excitement.

They'd said hello. There had been no need for introductions as they'd already known each other by name and sight. Damon had been a grade ahead of Bella, but she'd watched him from afar, attracted by his dark, slightly brooding good looks.

However, the meeting on the football field had been the first time they'd been completely alone, and Damon had been surprisingly friendly. Friendly in an easy, relaxed way. Not too smooth, and not obviously trying to chat her up. He'd walked with her across the playing field and then they'd stood leaning at the fence.

For ages. Just talking.

Suddenly she had been able to talk to this formidably sexy boy about practically anything.

They'd even talked about their parents—a subject that high-schoolers normally shunned. Bella had known Damon's dad was the new police sergeant and that they'd moved from Brisbane to Willara, so she'd asked if his dad was happy about the transfer.

Damon had been offhand. 'Sure he's happy. It's a good promotion and he gets to be the boss of a much bigger region.'

Even that first time, she'd sensed his tension when he spoke about his dad. He hadn't mentioned his mother at all, but she'd heard through the grapevine that she'd been killed in a car crash.

On that first afternoon, they'd also found common ground in being only children. Bella had admitted she was spoiled, and Damon had pulled a face as if that was a concept outside his experience.

Mostly, they'd smiled a lot. It had seemed they couldn't stop smiling, and Bella had been so thrilled to be sharing this conversation with him. She'd never felt so excited or over-the-moon happy. Just drinking in Damon's wild, rugged beauty and silver-grey eyes, she'd been sure she was floating.

Before they'd parted, he'd touched her just once, ever so briefly. His fingertips had skimmed light as moth wings over her wrist, electrifying her. Then he'd been gone, running back across the playing field, leaving her with an astonishing certainty that this was the start of something very important.

The police car stopped outside a nondescript grey weatherboard building on the edge of the highway and Bella was brought to the present with a sickening jolt. The station was surrounded by a surprisingly neat garden, enclosed by a chain-wire fence. Beyond the building on either side stretched bushland.

They were in the middle of nowhere.

Her stomach hollowed as she stepped out of the car. She swayed dizzily, and Damon put his arm around her shoulders, supporting her. His lips brushed her ear.

'Trust me,' he murmured softly. 'We'll be okay.'

She wanted to believe him. She had to believe him. Of course he hadn't stolen a car. Trusting him, she felt a little stronger.

The policeman led them up a narrow concrete path and unlocked the station door. Inside, there was a stark, utilitarian office with phones and two computers, a desk with two chairs.

'Sit here, please,' they were told sternly.

Silently, they sat, and Bella tried to draw steady breaths, in and out, to stop herself from panicking.

The policeman removed his cap to reveal a spiky ginger crew cut that made him look younger than ever. After hanging the cap on a peg, he pulled out a sheaf of official-looking paperwork and began to fill in details of their names and addresses, their dates of birth, today's date and the time. He consulted his computer.

The process was tedious and endless, and Bella had never felt so impatient, so desperate to be out of there.

At last the policeman looked up from his work. 'The

car you were driving shows up as stolen from the Gold Coast.'

No way. Bella wanted to shout their innocence.

Beside her, Damon spoke calmly. 'I have no idea what happened at the Gold Coast, but I hired the car in good faith. It was a legitimate deal. Ring the agency in Willara and ask them.'

The young constable narrowed his eyes, clearly displeased that he'd been told what to do. 'Wait here,' he snapped and he disappeared into the next room.

As soon as he was gone, Damon reached over and tweaked a stray strand of Bella's hair. 'We'll be okay,' he said softly. 'We'll be out of here in no time.'

'Maybe we should explain that we're worried about our grandparents?'

His lip curled and he shook his head. 'This guy wouldn't give a toss about our grandparents.'

'I don't like him,' Bella whispered.

'I'm afraid he doesn't care if you like him or not. He's a cop.'

Before they could say any more, the constable was back. 'I have no choice,' he said and the glimmer of a self-satisfied smirk pulled at the corners of his mouth. 'I'm going to have to arrest you both.'

A choked cry broke from Bella. Her head spun and she was only dimly aware of the rest of the policeman's speech…

Anything you say can be used as evidence… You may call a solicitor…

'But why?' she pleaded, her voice shaking with fear and indignation. 'We haven't done anything wrong.'

'Bella.'

She heard Damon's quiet, firm warning, but she was

too distressed to heed him. 'Damon hasn't stolen any-thing,' she shouted. 'We haven't stolen anything.' She rounded on the policeman. 'Surely the car agency at Willara told you we're innocent?'

'They're closed today,' the policeman said dismis-sively. 'Apparently, most of Willara township is at a big race meeting.'

Bella groaned, knowing this was true. Almost the entire Willara district came to a halt for their annual race day. Today of all days! Of all the rotten luck.

'I have sufficient reason to suspect that an offence has been committed.' The policeman cleared his throat and he shot a particularly vicious glance at Damon. 'You have a prior conviction for car theft.'

Oh, God. Bella saw the colour leave Damon's face, saw the muscles in his throat work overtime as he swallowed. Now she knew for certain that they had no chance of escaping this arrest.

Damon had assured her they'd be okay.

He was wrong.

His eyes blazed with anger. 'I was eighteen, for God's sake, and it was a suspended sentence.'

Bella jumped to his defence. 'The charge was unfair back then, and I can't believe you'd try to use a silly schoolboy prank as a reason to hold us now.'

Ignoring her, the policeman kept his eyes fixed on Damon. 'Do you admit you've committed a prior of-fence?'

'Yes.' Damon swallowed again. 'But Bella isn't in-volved. She didn't hire the car. I did.' His jaw tightened. 'And if you try to pin this on us, it'll backfire big time. Believe me.'

The policeman wasn't fazed. 'You want to call a lawyer?'

Damon turned to Bella. 'It's more important to call the hire-car people at Willara, but I doubt they'll be open before tomorrow.'

She nodded, too scared and too horrified to speak. She was thinking about her father and how shocked and devastated he would be if he knew she'd been arrested. She thought of Kent, her strong, reliable, protective fiancé until just a short day ago. Almost as soon as their engagement had ended, she'd thrown the security he'd represented to the four winds.

She'd convinced herself that the only reason she'd come on this journey was to rescue her grandfather, that the attraction of an old boyfriend played no part in her decision. But what use was she to Paddy now? She'd landed in deeper trouble than he'd probably encountered in his entire long life—apart, perhaps, from when he was a soldier on active service.

Damon Cavello's second name was Trouble. Why hadn't she remembered that? More importantly, why hadn't she been completely honest with herself? She should have admitted that her feelings for Damon had never died. If she'd accepted that painful truth at the start, she would never have risked coming away with him.

Watching Bella walk into her cell was the worst, the very worst moment of Damon's life. He wanted to roar with rage, wanted to scoop her up in his arms and race her out of there.

A crazy idea, of course. Impossible. And to launch a

verbal battle with the stubborn young constable would only make matters worse.

If their situation could be any worse.

For now, he and Bella were locked up in the tiny watch-house attached to the police station, one in each of the two cells. They were separated by a wall of bars, so that any policeman on duty could observe the two of them from his post.

Each cell had a bunk, a stainless-steel wash basin and a stainless-steel toilet bolted to the floor. A vent covered by security mesh was the only means of cooling. The midsummer's day was stifling hot.

Standing in the centre of his cell, Damon watched Bella walk to her bunk and sit carefully on its edge. She took off her cap, removed an elastic band, freeing her hair from its ponytail. Her hair fell to her shoulders in soft pale waves. Damon watched. She looked fragile. Delicate and beautiful. So brave. He knew it was fanciful, but she made him think of a fairy-tale princess locked in a tower.

She sent him a valiant little smile and waved to him. He tried to smile back, but he doubted he could cheer her. Then with a surprising air of purpose, she lay on her bunk, on her back with her arms by her sides and her eyes closed.

No doubt, she was probably trying to relax, which was sensible. At least she'd accepted that no one would wave a magic wand and set them instantly free. Damon admired her strength. After the stress she'd been under recently, with worries about her family and her broken engagement, this disaster must be the final straw. He hoped she was going to be okay.

His head was crammed with self-recriminations,

with what ifs and if onlys. But in reality, Damon knew he had few options. His one glimmer of hope was the fact that their arrest was based purely on suspicion. Surely, when the constable's superior turned up, their case would be investigated properly and the truth would be discovered.

In the meantime, he had no choice but to be patient. Which meant he should try to relax, too. Not easy when he was mad as hell and plagued by guilt. This bizarre predicament was his fault.

If only he hadn't had that prior conviction.

If only he'd asked the car-hire people more questions before he'd signed up for the damned car. If only he hadn't agreed to Bella coming on this trip.

But regrets were a waste of head space. Damon knew that, and normally he didn't give them the time of day. Right now, he couldn't get past them.

Lying on her bunk, eyes closed, breathing slowly, Bella tried to keep her fears at bay. She'd learned a little about meditation in yoga classes and now she tried to summon everything she knew about calming her whirling thoughts. She was trying to relax in the cloud pose.

Imagine I'm floating, soft and light as a cloud...

In almost no time her eyes flashed open. She tried several more times to 'float' without much luck.

Instinctively, she turned towards Damon's cell. He was sitting on the edge of his bunk, leaning forward, rubbing at his eyes with one hand. She knew he was tense, could see the strain in his shoulders and in the tendons standing out on his tanned forearms.

She remembered how closely those strong arms had held her once, remembered the blissful thrill of his lips on hers, the way his mouth had traced patterns of hot desire over her skin.

Without warning, her pleasant memories were over-shadowed by darker thoughts. She was reliving the time Damon was arrested, remembering how he'd been the talk of the town and her parents had forbidden her to see him again, even after he was released.

Oh, God, the pain of it. Using Kent as her messenger, she'd managed to smuggle a note to Damon, then she'd stolen out late at night for a secret tryst with him on the creek bank. She'd been determined to make love to him that night, but to her horror he'd told her it was over between them. He'd asked her to forget him.

Even now, the pain of that night brought tears to her eyes. At the time, no matter how hard she'd cried and protested Damon had insisted he was wrong for her.

The next day he'd gone away without making contact again. Bella had wanted to die.

She'd been such a mess.

Later, much, much later…she'd told herself that everyone suffered unbearable heartbreak over their first boyfriend. The longing for what you couldn't have was always the worst kind of hurt. In time, her broken heart had gradually healed, or at least she'd thought it had.

Yet here she was again, all these years later, lining up like an addict for another, dangerous dose of Damon Cavello.

As the day wore on the heat in the cells grew more intense and Damon's feelings of guilt grew heavier, squeezing the very air from his lungs.

Their situation was ludicrous. He and Bella had set out on this trip to find an elderly couple, who almost certainly couldn't cope alone with such a long journey. Charging like the cavalry, they'd come up the highway, ready to help, in any way necessary.

What a joke.

Silently, Damon let out a string of swear words, but he felt no better for it. He couldn't believe he'd allowed Bella to become once again entangled in his sorry, trouble-jinxed life.

Hadn't he caused her enough problems when they were young?

He'd been such a problem teenager, endlessly fighting with his heavy-handed father. Perhaps he should have recognised then that his old man had been badly hurt when his mother left. Easy to say now, but who could put a wise head on young shoulders?

At the time he'd been turbulent, questioning everything, and his dad had become increasingly strict. Instead of knuckling under and conforming, instead of going the please-the-parent route, like most kids… Damon had rebelled.

Once too often, as it turned out.

A movement in Bella's cell dragged him out of his dark memories. She'd risen from her bunk and was walking to the sink, where she filled a paper cup with water. As Damon watched her she turned and sent him a worried smile. She lifted her cup in a salute.

Despite the brave gesture, her green eyes were wide with fear, and her mouth was distorted as if she was battling not to cry. She came to the bars that separated their cells.

'I don't care if it's not allowed,' she whispered. 'I need to talk to you. I can't just sit here in the naughty corner until tomorrow.'

Wishing like hell that he weren't so helpless, Damon went over to her. A glance back to the window in the far door showed that their guard was currently elsewhere.

'I can't bear this,' Bella said, gripping the bars.

'You know we'll be okay.' He doubted he could reassure her, but he had to try. 'We just have to wait it out.'

'How can you be so patient?'

This was a surprise. He'd been worried he was setting her a bad example. 'I don't feel very patient. I feel like head-butting my way out through that concrete wall.'

'Well, you're acting very calm. I was half expecting you to flare up.'

'True to my reputation?'

She managed a small smile. 'I guess.'

'I'd like to think I've learned a thing or two since high school. I've been in enough bad situations I've finally worked out it's not worth provoking people in authority.'

Even so, Damon realised that his hands were gripping the bars so hard his knuckles were white. He was damn angry. 'I went out of my way to co-operate with this fellow. We would have been all right if I hadn't had that prior.'

'I think it's crazy to hold something like that against you now. You were too young.'

'In the eyes of the law I was an adult. I was eighteen.'

'Only just.'

Bella's pretty eyes brimmed with sympathy, a sympathy Damon was sure he didn't deserve. But she'd always been like that—concerned and understanding, always ready to defend him. In their teens, she'd been his good influence. Sweet and funny, she'd calmed him down.

He drew a sharp breath, wondering if she'd also been thinking about their past. He'd been so crazy in love with her then, and he'd never again felt that same rush, that sensational, over-the-top burst of passionate longing.

Hell. He shouldn't be remembering this…but he couldn't help recalling Bella's eagerness, the way she'd kissed like there was no tomorrow and begged him to make love to her. And yet…while he'd been wild in most other respects, with Bella he'd been cautious. He'd been worried about her reputation. In a tiny town like Willara, you couldn't buy condoms or get a prescription for the Pill without everyone knowing…

So he'd had it all carefully planned to be perfect… Then his ongoing war with his dad had ruined everything.

Damon fingered the puckered scar on the back of his right hand, a legacy from the time his dad had whipped off his police belt and whacked him hard, forgetting about the buckle end.

Bella was looking at the scar, too, and frowning. 'Where is your dad now?' she asked.

'Brisbane.'

'Still in the police force?'

He grimaced. 'Yeah. Unfortunately. No doubt he'll hear about this little escapade and it'll confirm his worst fears.'

She let out a huff of annoyance. 'I still can't believe the police are taking any notice of something that happened so long ago. I know you didn't want to tell that constable it was your father who arrested you, but it might have made a difference.'

'I doubt it.' Damon gritted his teeth. It was pointless to rake through the past, but now he wished he could reach back through the years and knock some sense into his teenage head.

Problem was, even when he'd turned eighteen, his father hadn't let up. In fact he'd become more of a stand-over merchant. He'd even put a stop to the eighteenth birthday party they'd planned.

'I never did understand how that other arrest happened,' Bella said. 'The last time we met—'

She stopped abruptly, clamped a hand to her mouth as her eyes glittered with sudden tears.

'Bell.' Damon's voice was choked as he remembered the pain of that last, desperately difficult meeting. He'd always known he'd hurt her—but he'd had no choice. It killed him to see that she'd carried the hurt all these years later.

'It's okay,' she said, blinking. 'I'm okay. It's just that I had to rely on Willara gossip back then to find out what had happened. Everyone was talking about it, but they all had different stories.'

Damon shot another glance back to the empty window in the far wall. 'It was the dumbest thing I ever did.'

'If it landed us here,' Bella said with gentle determination, 'I'd like to know what really happened.'

She gave a sad little smile, which he returned as best he could.

A sigh escaped him. 'You probably remember how mad I was with my old man for grounding me.'

'Yes, of course. I was mad, too. We had such a fabulous party planned.'

'Yeah. So the night after my birthday and the non-event party I simply grabbed the keys to a car Dad had impounded in the police yard, and I took it for a burn.'

Damon shook his head. 'Smart move, I know. Dad chased after me, of course, and brought me back, and we got into a row about how serious it was. I tried to make out there was no harm done, but I had to be a smart aleck. Said something stupid like I thought the family car was the only vehicle I wasn't allowed to drive.'

'That would have gone down well.' Bella rolled her eyes.

'Made him madder, of course. He puffed up like a strutting turkey and said he was going to teach me a lesson I'd never forget. He called the constable in and told him to book me for unlawful use of impounded property.'

Bella sighed and looked away. Damon half expected her to tell him that she would have known all these details if they hadn't split up so abruptly. Walking away from Bella Shaw was the hardest thing he'd ever done, but he'd known he had no choice. She was better off without him.

'But you were let off,' she said.

'Yeah—I defended myself in court. Showed remorse, and the magistrate gave me a suspended sentence.'

Thinking back on it, however, Damon knew that his old man had been right about one thing. He'd never forgotten that lesson. It was one of the reasons he was trying so damn hard to keep his cool now.

A noise behind them brought him whirling round. A tall, grey-haired senior sergeant strode through the watch-house doorway, with the constable trailing behind him, eyes lowered as he unhappily clutched a bunch of keys.

The older policeman went straight to Bella's cell. 'Good afternoon, Miss Shaw, I'm Senior Sergeant Jemison. Rod Jemison. I'd like to clarify a couple of matters relating to the car you were driving.'

'It's all been a terrible mistake.' Bella's voice shook as if tears weren't far away.

The senior sergeant frowned, then took a step back while the constable unlocked her door. 'Take a seat in my office, Miss Shaw,' he said quietly. 'I'll be with you in a moment.'

At last, Damon thought. Someone with authority. And this new senior officer hadn't told the constable to watch Bella, so he clearly didn't see her as a fugitive. He'd offered his first name, too, which had to be a friendly overture. Things were looking up.

So play it cool, Cavello...

'Mr Cavello.' Through the metal bars, the officer fixed Damon with intelligent blue eyes. 'One quick question.'

'If it's about my prior—'

The other man held up a hand to silence him. 'It's much simpler than that. Are you the Cavello who sends news reports from Afghanistan and the Middle East?'

Damon nodded. 'My press pass is in the wallet your constable confiscated.'

Rod Jemison shot his constable a sharp, sideways glance. 'Get him out of there, while I sort this out.'

Half an hour later, Bella and Damon were once again standing on the edge of the highway.

Seesawing between emotional exhaustion and an up-rush of relief, Bella thought her knees might give way. Even so, she couldn't hold back a grin.

'Free at last!' she shouted, then laughed at her exuberance. 'Anyone would think I'd been incarcerated for months instead of half a day.'

To her surprise, Damon slipped an arm around her shoulders, gave her a hug, even brushed a soft kiss on her cheek. 'I'm sorry. You shouldn't have had to go through that.'

His kiss was gentle, hardly touching her, yet Bella could feel it vibrating all the way through her. 'Don't feel bad. I'm fine,' she said, sending him a shaky smile. 'At least I am now it's all over.'

The temptation to give Damon an answering kiss was overwhelming. She wanted to be impulsive, to wind her arms around his neck and lose herself in kissing him—the way they used to.

Don't go there. Don't get carried away. Just in time she remembered all the reasons she had to hold back. Damon would leave again soon, just as he'd left last time. She'd had enough problems recently. She couldn't risk more.

Instead she told him, 'You were right, Damon. We just had to be patient.'

Their release had been unbelievably quick once the senior sergeant had taken charge. They'd been asked to sit in the office, and Damon had explained yet again that he'd hired the car from a service station in Willara, and that he'd paid with his credit card.

In response, Sergeant Jemison had used his mobile phone to dial straight through to his Willara counterpart, who was, sure enough, at the races.

Within a matter of minutes, an announcement for the car-hire agent had been broadcast over the racecourse PA, the fellow had been located, and he'd confirmed that Damon rented the car legitimately and in good faith. Apparently two backpackers with very poor English had hired the car at the Gold Coast and driven it for several days beyond their time limit before abandoning it at Willara, because, technically, it was a stolen car.

The car-hire fellow in Willara had been slack with his paperwork and the car had shown up in the police system as stolen. But it was soon very clear that Bella and Damon had been innocent victims.

So now they were officially innocent and standing on the edge of the highway, in the middle of nowhere, with no mode of transport.

Bella had half expected an apology from the police, but the sergeant was quite firm.

'You were pulled up in a stolen vehicle and one of you had form,' he'd said. 'Of course you had to be detained and I have to impound the car until this is sorted out.'

'You mean we're stuck here?' she'd cried, horrified.

'I can drive you back to Rockhampton first thing in the morning, and you'll be able to hire another car there. But for tonight, I'm afraid your best bet is the motel down the road.'

Not a great option, Bella thought as she eyed the drab, rather faded nest of buildings on the far side of a dusty paddock. It was now late afternoon, but the sun was still very fierce and the motel's metal roof was baking in the sun.

'I hope it has air conditioning,' she said as she hefted her bag over her shoulder.

Damon nodded. 'Air conditioning and a good mattress and we'll be ready to face the world again.'

'Two good mattresses,' Bella corrected.

His eyes flashed as their gazes connected, and she felt a fierce jolt in the centre of her chest.

'Two mattresses, of course,' he said with a quiet, unreadable smile.

'In separate rooms.'

'That shouldn't be a problem. By the look of this place, we'll be the only guests.'

CHAPTER FIVE

DAMON was wrong.

The motel was, they soon discovered, a favourite, low-budget stopover for truck drivers and travelling salesmen. Although most of the patrons hadn't arrived yet, the place was almost fully booked out for the evening. There was just one vacancy.

'Are you sure there's nothing else?' Bella winced at how nervous she sounded, but she was practically hyperventilating at the thought of sharing a room with Damon.

'Just the one room, but we can offer you an extra-large room with twin beds.' The motel proprietor's tone implied they were exceptionally lucky to be offered this and should be excessively grateful.

Damon set an extra hundred-dollar bill on the counter. 'Are you quite certain you can't find another room for Miss Shaw?'

The proprietor eyed the bribe forlornly and his fingers twitched as if he longed to take it. 'Honestly, mate, I'd love to help, but apart from that one room we're chock-a-block tonight.'

Damon frowned. 'Is there any other accommodation around here?'

'The next motel's another hundred clicks up the high-way. I can ring them if you like—'

'Thanks, but we'll be fine here,' Bella cut in, ignoring Damon's frown. They had no transport and this motel room was their only option.

Besides, she was embarrassed about making a fuss over sharing the room. For heaven's sake, she was a mature, twenty-first-century woman not a nervous virgin in a Jane Austen novel. 'The twin room will be lovely,' she said, flashing a confident smile. 'Thank you.'

Chin high, she avoided meeting Damon's gaze. No doubt he was amused by their new situation.

'Do you serve meals?' she asked.

'Sure, miss. The breakfast menus are in your rooms. Dinner's at seven in the dining room. I think it's a roast tonight.'

They were handed the keys and as they left Reception Bella couldn't help thinking about the many women Damon had shared rooms with in heaven knew how many countries. Her own experience was rather limited. She hadn't had many boyfriends.

It wasn't for lack of trying, but for some reason she'd never really fallen deeply in love, and she'd rarely got to the stage of going away for a weekend with a boyfriend. There'd been one dismal attempt when the guy in question had forgotten to mention he was a mad keen golfer.

He'd booked a resort with a golf course, and he'd disappeared with his clubs from breakfast till dinner, and Bella had been bored out of her tree. The evenings hadn't gone well, either.

On tenterhooks now, she took a deep breath as Damon pushed open the door.

The room was as faded and worn as she'd expected, and the furnishings were out-of-date ugly, rather than attractively old-fashioned, but any motel room was a darned sight better than the police lockup.

Sinking onto one of the beds, she was suddenly exhausted by their ordeal. Sitting in a cell and doing nothing had totally worn her out. Until, that was, a quick glance at the dark, broad-shouldered male sauntering past the end of her bed wiped her tiredness in a blink, and replaced it with a brand-new edginess.

Damon, naturally, looked totally relaxed as he made himself at home, unpacking his duffle bag, putting his shaving gear in the bathroom, plugging in his mobile phone to recharge, filling the electric kettle.

Too late, Bella realised she'd been feasting her eyes on him. So not a good start.

To distract herself she made phone calls to her father and Kent. Not the easiest of calls, given that she wanted to dodge any hint of their brush with the law and she hated lying. However, her dad reassured that he was really well, which was great news. And although he hadn't heard from Paddy, he was confident he could find out the name of her grandfather's old army mate in Port Douglas.

'I'll ring you as soon as I've got it,' he promised.

When Bella contacted Kent he reassured her that the wedding cancellations had been pretty much smooth sailing.

'Thanks to Zoe Weston's help,' he added.

Bella was intrigued by the warmth in Kent's voice when he spoke about Zoe, and she wondered if there could be an attraction growing between her two closest friends.

She might have brooded over Kent and Zoe some more if she hadn't been dealing with her own attraction issues. Despite her best intentions, she felt a deeper connection with Damon after their shared trouble with the police. Not unlike the bond she'd felt all those years ago. The two of them against the world.

The feeling both scared and excited her. She knew jolly well that there was absolutely no point in falling for Damon again. He'd come home to Australia on a flying visit to attend the wedding and to see his grandmother. Very soon he'd be gone again, disappearing overseas for another decade or more. Allowing her old feelings for Damon to resurface was a useless and dangerous exercise.

After all, when it came to choosing boyfriends or, for that matter, fiancés, her track record was pretty poor.

Just the same, the sad truth was her fears about sharing this room with him were caused more by her own vulnerability than a concern that Damon would try to seduce her. Just the intimacy of sleeping in a bed next to Damon Cavello and sharing a bathroom with him were enough to set her brain racing down all kinds of wrong tracks.

One minute she was thinking that a fling would be nice—just for old times' sake. Next she was reminding herself that, inevitably, her emotions would come to the party and she'd end up in a worse mess than ever.

It was rather maddening that Damon was ultra cool about their situation.

'Coffee?' he asked as Bella finished her phone calls.

She nodded gratefully. 'Thanks.'

'With milk and one sugar?'

'Yes, please. You have a very good long-term memory.'

'Nothing long-term about it. I don't think you even drank coffee when I knew you before.'

'Actually, you're right. I didn't. I was still addicted to milkshakes. So how did you know how I take my coffee?'

His eyes twinkled. 'Breakfast this morning.'

Duh. 'And you were taking notes, I suppose?'

'A good journalist has to be sharp-eyed, like a good detective.'

He handed her a steaming mug of coffee, and held out a little packet of biscuits. 'I'll let you have the one with the chocolate-cream filling.'

'That's very generous, Damon, but no, thanks. I couldn't manage it. I'm still trying to digest those door-stop sandwiches they gave us at the police station.' The thick corned beef and pickle sandwiches had settled heavily in Bella's stomach.

Setting his mug on the nightstand beside his bed, Damon kicked off his shoes, then lounged on top of the striped cotton bedspread, legs stretched in front of him and crossed at the ankles. He was wearing grey-and-black chequered socks that hugged the shape of his feet.

There was something incredibly private and domesti-cated about a man in socks, Bella thought. She dragged her gaze away from his feet. 'So tell me. What else have your sharp journalistic eyes observed?'

'You love wearing fancy nail polish.'

Her hands curled instinctively. Nail polish was her *thing.* Didn't Damon like it? 'I didn't mean observations about me.'

Over the rim of his coffee cup, he eyed her levelly. 'What do you want then? My observations about global warming? World peace? The state of Queensland's highways?'

She rolled her eyes to the ceiling. 'You're still a smart aleck, Damon Cavello.'

'And you're still gutsy, Bella Shaw.'

His praise was so unexpected her cheeks began to burn.

'I was so proud of the way you handled yourself today,' Damon said with surprising warmth.

'But I was petrified.'

'It didn't show.'

Something—a certain spark in his eyes—made her heart do a slow tumble turn. 'I took my cue from you, Damon.'

Their gazes linked and held, and Bella could feel an electric charge leaping between them.

Or was that her imagination getting carried away?

She looked down at her hands. 'I mean…I knew you must have experienced all kinds of dangerous situations…a lot worse than what happened to us today.'

'That's true.' He traced the rim of his coffee mug with his thumb. 'I've had a few close calls.'

'Have you been hurt?'

'Not as badly as a couple of my colleagues, but I did get nicked by a sniper's bullet once.'

'Ouch.' Bella flinched. The thought of a bullet hitting Damon anywhere horrified her.

'I was lucky,' he said with a quick grin. 'It grazed me across the arm.' He touched the top of his biceps. 'I was only out of action for a few days.'

'You make light of it, but I've read horrifying stories about foreign correspondents. About them being detained and imprisoned. Your work really is danger- ous, isn't it?'

'It can be...'

After a slight hesitation he said, 'In some places if you're detained, there's always a risk of being sold on to the highest bidder who will ransom you, or worse.'

'Oh, God.' A flare of hot panic ripped through Bella. 'That couldn't happen to you, could it?'

Frowning, Damon pinched the bridge of his nose between a thumb and forefinger.

She guessed he was considering the best way to an- swer her. 'Don't pull your old trick of covering up the bad stuff with a joke, Damon. I can handle the truth. Have you been in that kind of danger?'

'Not often.'

'But it's happened?'

He let out a heavy sigh. 'There was one time I was definitely going down that track. I was lucky. My driver, who was also my interpreter, was incredibly coura- geous. He had family contacts, and he dropped enough names and was so insistent that I only ended up paying a substantial fine, and I was able to continue.'

Bella drew a long, deep breath and let it out slowly. It was beyond awful to realise Damon had come so close... 'How do you cope, living with danger on an almost daily basis?'

She'd told him she could handle this subject. She hoped he couldn't see how rattled she was.

Damon's broad shoulders rose in an offhand shrug. 'I try to stay aloof.'

'Detached?'

'Yes. Especially in a war zone. As soon as you start

to take sides you're asking for serious trouble. A foreign correspondent has to be impartial. If you don't focus on that, you're soon caught out.'

'So you have to suppress your emotions. All the time.' Something Damon was very good at, Bella thought.

An awkward silence descended and Bella couldn't think of anything to say. She looked down at the final inch of coffee in her mug, sipped it and discovered that it had gone cold.

She supposed it was time to change the subject. 'You must be exhausted after driving all night,' she suggested. 'Would you like to take a little nap before dinner?'

'Hell, no.' Damon leapt from the bed as if it were electrified. 'I'm not your grandfather, Bella.'

He looked down at her, reminding her again of just how broad-shouldered and rugged he was. And then he grinned at her. 'But I'll take a shower.'

Which left Bella to lie there on her bed, flushed from the surprising warmth of Damon's sudden smile, and trying not to think about him stripping naked and showering on the other side of a very thin wall.

She buried her face in her pillow.

Dinner in the dining room was very ordinary. The room was too brightly lit and it was crowded with a dozen or more tired-looking salesmen who were either sitting alone with their newspapers, or chatting in small groups while downing the tall glasses of beer that accompanied their dry, overcooked roast.

Bella was the only female in the room, and with her

bright green eyes and golden hair she was a pretty butterfly amidst a crowd of dull moths.

She'd changed into slim white trousers and a soft green-and-aqua top in a floaty, feminine fabric, the kind of top that kept a man thinking about what lay beneath....

He pictured her in a romantic setting...at the edge of a tropical sea, perhaps, where whispering palm trees were silhouetted against the sky, and a gentle, balmy breeze brought the scent of frangipani. Their table would be covered with a crisp white damask cloth and positioned as close as possible to the water.

There'd be iced champagne and mouth-watering, freshly caught seafood, delicately spiced and cooked to perfection. A selection of tropical fruit for dessert.

They'd watch the moon come up over the sea and—

'A penny for your thoughts.'

Damon blinked. Bella was looking at him with a bemused smile and he wondered if she'd asked him a question.

'Sorry, I'm being very bad company. My mind was—ah—miles away.'

'In Afghanistan, I suppose, or the Middle East?'

'A bit of both,' he lied. 'It's a bad habit.'

'Thinking too much about work?' Bella shrugged. 'That's one problem I don't have right now. I've resigned from my job.'

'When you thought you were going to be a farmer's wife?'

Her lips tilted in a small, self-deprecating smile. 'Exactly.'

Perhaps unwisely, Damon said, 'I have to admit, I could never picture you in that role.'

'No, I don't suppose you could. When you knew me I had very different plans.'

'What were they?'

He saw a flash of pain in her eyes, the hasty biting of her lower lip before she swiftly looked down at her plate and began to cut her meat with the concentration of a brain surgeon. Eventually she said, with a forced, airy brightness, 'I can't remember *exactly* what I had planned back then.'

Damon knew she was lying and he felt a surge of guilt, remembering his abrupt departure from Willara and Bella's tears. He'd had to get away and he couldn't have taken her with him. He was wrong for her.

He was still wrong for her. She wanted a secure, settled life.

'I don't ever remember you talking about becoming a journalist,' Bella said, deftly changing the subject. 'How did that happen?'

Damon shrugged. 'Violet rang me when the Year Twelve results came through, and I found out I'd miraculously managed to score a place at university. I'm not sure why I chose to study journalism. I think I liked the idea of discovering new stories every day.'

'A bit like discovering what's around the next bend in the road?'

'Yes, I guess so.'

'But how could you afford university, and living away from home?'

'I managed to defer the fees, and I got myself two part-time jobs. One behind a bar, and another as a kitchen hand. A mate let me rent a spare bed in his grotty flat.'

'Was it hard to make the jump from journalism graduate to foreign correspondent?'

'I think I was lucky. Lots of journalists want to be foreign correspondents, so it's very competitive. But I headed straight overseas when I graduated, so by the time I applied for the foreign post I'd already worked on papers in Singapore and Hong Kong. I'd made a lot of contacts, and that proved to be a handy foot in the door.'

'I can understand why you like it. You get to cover all the really big stories. War, famine, earthquakes.'

'Yeah…it's a tad more exciting than reporting on the local school fête.'

Bella's response was a sad smile that chilled him to the bone. More than ever he was aware of the different paths their lives had taken after he'd left her behind.

'Now you can make new plans,' he suggested. 'You can start a new chapter.'

'Yes, but my problem is I don't actually see any clear role for me now.'

'Will you look for another job?'

'Probably, but I don't want to make any plans until we find Paddy and Violet and get them safely home.'

'Now *that* is *my* responsibility,' he said. 'You shouldn't have to worry, Bella. I'm confident we'll have smooth sailing from here.'

'Don't say that too loudly. The gods might hear you.'

Damon could see she was almost serious. No surprise, really, given everything that had happened to her. 'Let's be optimistic,' he suggested.

'You're right.' She shrugged and gave a sheepish smile. 'I used to be optimistic, but somehow I seem to have lost the knack.'

'You've had a lot to worry about, and it's all been other people's troubles. Now it's time to plan for things you want.'

'I'm sure you're right.' She didn't sound hopeful.

Determined to cheer her, Damon raised his glass. 'Here's to happier times ahead.'

Letting her glass clink against his, Bella smiled. 'Yep. Here's to happier times. I'll hold that thought.' She took a sip, then set the glass down again. 'There's always travel. Zoe and I were planning to travel before the engagement. It would be great if she's still interested.'

'Well, if you decide to travel, I'm your man. I can offer you all kinds of advice.'

'I suppose you've been to every country.'

'Almost.'

'Zoe and I might have to consult you,' she said, almost coyly. 'How much do you charge for your travel advice?'

They walked back to their motel room, down a dimly lit path, where occasional garden lamps afforded Bella tempting glimpses of Damon's gorgeous profile. She knew this meal hadn't been anything remotely close to a date. But just being around Damon again made her feel all wistful and wanting.

There'd been moments when Damon had looked at her across the table when she'd wanted to leap out of her chair and into his lap.

Other times she'd felt horribly depressed, as if her whole life had been one huge stuff-up and she'd missed out every step of the way. Damon, meanwhile, had fixed his eyes on a goal and gone after it.

Let's be optimistic...he'd said.

Right now her most optimistic thought involved kissing him.

Making love...

A whole night lay ahead of them...a fantasy waiting to happen...

Here she was, all grown up and alone with her high-school sweetheart for one long night in a motel room in the middle of nowhere. No chance for meddlesome gossip.

And the bonus was—Damon was even more attractive than he'd been in his bad-boy youth. Maturity hadn't just given him broader shoulders and an air of confidence, he was worldly and experienced, with a brooding, mysterious aura that made him disturbingly sexy.

He was still as dangerous as ever, of course.

That was the hitch. Bella was all too aware of the risks. If she gave in to her impulses with Damon tonight, she had to accept that he would break her heart again.

They'd left one lamp on in their room, and its soft yellow glow made the furnishings look less faded.

Damon dropped the keys on a bedside table and reached for the TV remote. 'Do you want to catch a little TV before we hit the hay?'

'TV?' Bella's mind was on a completely different track. In fact, she'd been so carried away, she'd almost convinced herself that she could risk a fling with Damon and deal with the emotional fallout later.

Okay, yesterday she'd been determined to remain a flirtation-free zone, but tonight she had to ask how, in heaven's name, she could keep up that façade when every cell in her body screamed to be in Damon's arms?

She didn't want to listen to boring common sense. She'd devoted enough time to duty and to doing the right thing and right now she didn't want to dwell on the emotional consequences of such rashness. Emotions could be such a nuisance. Life would be so much simpler without them.

Tonight she was brimming with memories of Damon's kisses all those years ago. Perhaps, if they'd consummated their love back then, she wouldn't be burning with lust and curiosity now. But they'd waited in their teens. They'd actually had it all planned—they'd even bought condoms from a pharmacy out of town— but then Damon had been arrested.

End of story.

Tonight Bella ached to discover the new Damon, the sexy, experienced man of the world. Over dinner this evening there'd been several times when she'd seen a flash in his eyes that had been so fierce and fiery it had lit a thousand firecrackers inside her.

But how could she expect him to guess she was interested after the huge fuss she'd made about separate rooms?

Right now, Damon was standing with his finger poised on the remote, waiting for her answer. What could she say? *No, I have a better idea. Why don't we start ripping each other's clothes off?*

Bella sighed, and wished she'd had more experience with casual sex. 'Sure,' she said, despondently realising she was not going to magically turn into a femme fatale. 'Put the TV on. I'll—um—make a cup of tea.' She headed towards the kettle. 'Would you like one?'

'No, thanks.' A popular mystery series flickered onto the screen and Damon made himself comfortable, removing his shoes and socks, slipping the belt from his jeans, untucking his shirttails and letting them hang free.

Of course, Bella imagined slipping her hands under his shirt and exploring his hard, satiny muscles. *Oh, man.*

She wondered again if she should try to signal her new mood. Should she stand in front of the TV and do a slow striptease? Sit on the edge of Damon's bed and undo his shirt buttons? Just grab the remote and tell him straight out what she wanted?

For her, there was nothing else in this room but a six-foot-tall, shockingly sexy male.

Damon's eyes, however, were focused on the television. He flicked the remote, surfing channels till he came to a news story set overseas. There'd been a car bomb, apparently, and officials were being questioned. His attention was captured.

No longer relaxed, he sat up, leaning forward, face intent, frowning, pointing at the screen. 'That guy's a murderer. He's wormed his way into security. I know him. Damn it, he's playing both sides. And they're not asking the right questions.'

It was another facet of the new Damon. A man she no longer knew, a man whose interests lay in countries that were oceans away, in societies she didn't understand.

Even as she thought this Damon jumped up and started to pace the room, his eyes still fixed on the screen where a man in dark glasses was being questioned and giving his assurance that the bombers would be quickly tracked down and arrested.

Damon groaned, quickly snatched up his mobile and began to dial. 'Greg, it's Damon. Yes, Damon Cavello. Yes, I'm still in Australia. Listen, are you monitoring Channel Twelve?'

Without a glance in Bella's direction, Damon made his way to the door. 'Well, get on to it,' he said as he pushed the door open and stepped out. 'They're letting the "Grasshopper" off the hook. Surely they must know the truth about this bloke.'

The door closed behind him and reality hit Bella like several buckets of cold water. How could she, the girl Damon left behind, the girl who'd never been to university, and who'd never left Queensland, hope to re-capture his interest?

Stifling a sigh, she switched on the kettle, angry that she'd let her foolish fantasies take hold. Damon was be-having true to form and he was keeping the promise he'd made when she'd agreed to come away with him.

Okay, maybe he had looked at her with unmistak-able interest, but that was probably his modus operandi with most single women.

She might as well make coffee, not tea. She was going to be awake all night anyway.

CHAPTER SIX

LYING in the dark, mere feet away from Bella, and pretending to be asleep, Damon endured—no contest—the worst night of his life. It mightn't have been quite so bad if Bella wasn't as restless as he was, but she was tossing and turning like someone in a fever. At times she even threw off the sheets offering Damon a perfect, moonlit view of her.

He could see her hair shining like a pale river of silk on the pillow, her hips curving enticingly beneath her thin cotton nightshirt, her shapely legs, sleek and smooth. Ripe for touching.

If he'd shared a room with any other woman he would, almost certainly, have bedded her by now, broken engagement notwithstanding. In many cases, a romantic disappointment had proved an incentive.

But Damon wasn't taking any risks with Bella's heart.

Not again.

He knew he'd hurt her last time, but he'd been sure she got over that long ago. Tonight, however, talking about the steps he'd taken to set himself up with an interesting career, he'd seen the lost, lonely look in her eyes, and he'd felt like a traitor, a selfish jerk.

If only she knew how it had killed him to walk away from her. He'd done it for her own good, had been convinced she was better off without him. But tonight... he'd been forced to see that she wasn't happy.

If anyone deserved happiness, Bella did. But what could he do?

He couldn't offer her any more emotional security now than he could at eighteen. He was a long-term outsider, an observer. A gypsy forever on the move. He enjoyed women's company from time to time, but he always moved on.

Besides...sex with Bella could never be casual...

Not for him...

If they slept together now, and then he left again, they would only stir up deeply buried anguish. His scars and hers.

Why invite pain?

No. It was best to stay clear.

Stifling a deep urge to sigh, Damon rolled over, closed his eyes and tried to ignore the powerful signals that his body was primed for action.

His plan to relax might have worked. He might have cleared his head of any thoughts of the long-ago sweetheart lying so close beside him if her bed hadn't creaked, and if he hadn't heard an even deeper, more wretched sigh from her.

Unable to curb his curiosity, he turned a few degrees, and opened one eye.

Bella was sitting on the edge of her bed. A patch of moonlight made a silver halo of her hair and outlined her shoulders and the shape of her breasts through the thin fabric of her nightshirt.

'What's the matter?' he asked more gruffly than he'd meant to.

'Sorry,' she whispered. 'I didn't mean to wake you.'

'Are you okay?'

'Yes. I'm fine. I'm just having trouble getting to sleep.'

You and me both. 'Would it—ah—help if I turned down the air conditioning?'

'No, it's not too hot.'

'Do you need a drink of water?'

'I've got one, thanks.' With an unconsciously graceful motion, Bella lifted her hair away from the back of her neck and gave it a little twist. Then she let it fall again. Beneath her nightshirt, her breasts rose and fell in intoxicating unison.

Had she no idea?

Or was she deliberately trying to drive him crazy?

Damon closed his eyes, pretending to be sleepy. The alternative was to leap up and haul her into his arms, to bury his face in the warm, sweet-smelling curve of her neck, to let his hands reach beneath her flimsy nightwear.

'Damon?'

'Yes?'

'Do you ever wonder what it might have been like if we'd—you know—gone all the way?'

He jolted upright, heart pumping, fighting for air, breaths coming in ragged bursts. He stared at her in dismay.

Finally, he managed to speak. 'What kind of question is that?'

A burning one, he thought, answering himself.

Bella didn't reply, but he knew she was watching

him. Her face was in shadow and he couldn't see her expression. He fervently hoped she couldn't see his.

But perhaps she did see something in his face. Suddenly, she let out a little cry and covered her face with her hands. 'I'm so sorry. I can't believe I asked you that.'

He wanted to leap out of bed, to gather her in to him. Wanted to kiss her from head to toe, to strip her nightshirt from her and make love with blinding passion and aching sensitivity. Wanted to lose himself and find himself. In her.

At the very least, he wanted to reassure her that he understood her question and her need to voice it. It was the same question that had burned inside him for ten years.

As young lovers he and Bella had been wildly passionate and inventive, and so many times, they'd come to the brink of the final act. But in a small, gossipy country town like Willara a guy had to be so careful. While Damon had been reckless about his own safety, with Bella he'd been super-careful.

He'd planned and he'd waited with excruciating impatience…and then he'd wrecked everything…and it was too late.

Now, here she was, asking: *Do you ever wonder what it might have been like?*

And, God help him, here *they* were, consenting adults alone in a motel room. All he had to do was reach out. Touch her. And she would be his. He'd never desired another woman the way he wanted Bella.

If he was honest he would tell her: *yes, I've wondered and I've regretted a thousand times.*

Instead he remained silent and Bella sat very still

for a very long time. Damon wished he knew what she was thinking and feeling. Was she crying? He was desperate to turn on the light, to see the expression on her face. His hand hovered by the light switch.

'I'm really sorry,' she said at last. 'From the moment I heard you were coming back, I was determined that I mustn't try to revisit the past. I don't know what came over me. I just started wondering—what if things had worked out—differently? Please, Damon—can you forget what I said?'

It was his chance to be honest, to tell Bella his regrets.

But it was too late. He was a different man now. They'd both changed, and for months now Bella had been under a great deal of strain. Her plans to travel with Zoe were on the right track—far safer than conversations in the dark about sex and regrets and lost possibilities...

Damon cleared his throat. 'Sure. There's no use digging up the past. I won't give it another thought.'

To his surprise, Bella accepted this without comment. She lay down again and pulled the covers up tightly under her chin, and once she was settled she didn't move. Eventually, Damon heard her steady breathing and knew she was asleep.

His chances of following her example were zero.

Bella woke to a knock on the door and the arrival of the breakfast tray. As she struggled up onto one elbow, she saw Damon coming from the bathroom, already dressed and in the middle of shaving. As he came to the door and collected the tray one half of his jaw was covered in white lather, while the other half was smooth and tanned and ultra masculine.

Remembering last night and her stupid gaffe, she cringed. Oh, God, how on earth had she let that question out? What must Damon think of her?

The only way she could ever forgive herself was to cling to the excuse that she'd been totally thrown by the scary ordeal of being locked up. Even so, she might have stayed hiding under the covers if the aroma of freshly brewed coffee hadn't been so enticing.

'Good morning.' Damon's greeting was bright and breezy as he set her tray on the nightstand beside her. 'Coffee and grainy toast. That's what you ordered, isn't it?'

'Yes, that's lovely, thanks.' She couldn't quite meet his eyes and was grateful she was able to hide beneath her sleep-tumbled hair.

'We don't have a great deal of time,' he said. 'The senior sergeant will be here at eight-thirty.'

His tone had shifted to businesslike and Bella wondered if he was as keen as she was to pretend that last night's silly question had never been raised. Slightly cheered by this possibility, she sat up and reached for her coffee pot.

Just then, her mobile phone rang.

'It's from my father,' she said, picking up the phone. 'Oh, good news. It's a text message with the name and address of Paddy's old army mate in Port Douglas.'

'Fantastic. Perhaps we should give them a call?'

'It might be a bit early for elderly people. I'll try mid morning.'

'Sure. That's fine.'

Already, Damon was tucking into his breakfast and

Bella was grateful that he behaved as if her embarrassing question hadn't bothered him in the slightest. She was so grateful now that she hadn't said more about her generally unhappy experiences with boyfriends.

All in all, they'd reached a sensible position. It was best to leave their past well behind them… Last night's small problem was unlikely to rise again. From here on they'd be sure to have separate rooms.

Their personal issues were behind them.

Senior Sergeant Rod Jemison was in a talkative mood as he drove Damon and Bella back to Rockhampton. He was keen for Damon to sit beside him and, as Bella was adamant that she was happy to sit alone in the back, he had little choice.

Once they took off, however, Rod Jemison said cheerfully to Damon, 'So, can you fill me in about your father?'

Momentarily, Damon considered asking him to stop the car right there and let him out. It wasn't an option, of course, and he was grateful for his years of practice at hiding his innermost thoughts and feelings. Just the same, he suspected the sergeant had sensed his negative reaction.

'I served with your father,' Rod Jemison continued. 'In fact, I spent five years working with Jack Cavello.'

'Yes, well…' Damon cleared his throat. 'We don't see much of each other these days, so there's a chance you know more about my old man than I do.'

The sergeant nodded, happy to talk about the places where he and Jack Cavello had been stationed together. He even told a couple of funny stories.

Then, without warning, he said, 'Jack's very proud of you, you know.'

Bloody hell. Just in time, Damon choked back a protest. The poor, deluded policeman probably thought he was saying the right thing, but he had no idea.

Jemison shot Damon a piercing, sideways glance. 'I've seen the scrapbooks—and the DVDs.'

'I'm sorry.' Damon swallowed a fiery rock that had lodged in his throat. 'I—uh—don't know what you're talking about.'

'The scrapbooks with all your news stories. And your TV reports. Jack's taped the lot and stored them on DVDs.'

'I think you must be mistaken.'

'No mistake, Damon. I've seen them. Jack made me sit down in his lounge room and look at the scrapbooks while he gave me chapter and verse about you.'

'He did?' Damon's question was little more than a whisper.

This was impossible. His dad couldn't have taken that much interest. He couldn't have cared. A tidal wave littered with buried emotions rushed over him. He couldn't speak, couldn't move, could barely breathe.

Rod Jemison was watching him. 'Have I surprised you?'

Surprised? Damon had been less shocked the time he'd been hit by a sniper's bullet.

'Yes, I'm surprised,' he managed at last. 'My father and I didn't—ah—*don't* get on. As I said, I haven't seen him for quite a—while.'

'I knew you two didn't see eye to eye when you were young,' the other man said quietly. 'But I assumed Jack had smoothed things out between you.'

Not a chance, Damon thought morosely, but he remained silent, his thoughts whirling with memories of his father's dark, angry face as he loomed over him, strap in hand. Or the way his father had stood to attention by the door of the courthouse, never meeting his son's eyes as he faced the magistrate. And then an earlier, even more painful memory of eating meals in unbearable silence while a cold war raged between his parents.

Like his mother, he'd been glad to escape.

'I know there were problems,' Rod Jemison continued. 'It's well known in our circles that Jack Cavello charged his own son for joy-riding. The interesting thing is he never regretted it, because you became so successful. He was so damn proud you turned out so well.'

Damon's face flamed uncomfortably. There was nothing he could say. He was fighting anger and despair in equal parts and damn near crying. The danger of breaking down appalled him.

The older man went on. 'It's not unusual for fathers in the police force to be too strict with their own kids. It's so easy for youngsters to go off the rails and sometimes they never come back. That's the fear of all fathers, especially policemen.'

At the cost of estrangement from their sons, Damon thought miserably.

By now they were back in Rockhampton again, sweeping over the bridge that crossed the Fitzroy River. In a matter of moments, Sergeant Jemison was pulling up outside a car-hire agency. Damon emerged from the police car, feeling dazed and pummelled, as if he were staggering, defeated, from a boxing bout with a world heavyweight champion.

His head was reeling with images of scrapbooks filled with his news stories, of DVDs, compiled, no doubt, with his father's typically methodical care. Without warning, he was seized by an emotion so deep and melancholy, it seemed to tear at his soul.

Somehow, he managed to thank Rod Jemison for the lift, and as the police car took off once more he was aware of Bella standing on the footpath beside him. He turned to her and saw that her eyes were brimming with shimmery tears.

She'd heard everything, of course, and more than anyone she could understand how shocked and shaken he was. Without saying a word, she reached for his hand.

Her fingers were cool and slender and Damon grasped them tightly. She stepped closer, her lovely face eloquently distorted with emotion. It was almost as if they'd been caught in a time warp, as if they'd gone back to a past where they were once again a special unit— just the two of them together, against the world.

With no thought for the passing traffic or curious shoppers, Damon opened his arms and drew her to him. Eyes closed, holding back tears, he wrapped her tightly against him.

He'd never needed anyone the way he needed Bella now. She, alone, could save him from drowning.

This time when Bella and Damon once again headed north, they were in a sturdy, all-wheel-drive station wagon, and Bella was aware of a distinct shift in their mood. Sergeant Jemison's disclosure about Damon's father had opened the door on their past, releasing emotions like moths from a dark closet.

Her heart wept for Damon. He'd always acted so tough, as if he didn't need or want his father's affection, but today he'd been forced to accept that his bonds to his dad had never been completely severed.

Bella could only guess at the shock he'd felt when he'd heard that his father had loved him from afar and in secret. The Cavello family ties were as deeply buried and twisted as old tree roots, but the emotions were real and alive. And painful.

Damon had trembled as he'd clung to her, as if something deep inside him had cracked open. And in that poignant, heartbreaking embrace, she hadn't only felt the raw honesty of his pain, but she'd sensed his need for her—as strong and powerful as ever—as if he'd taken an irreversible step closer to her.

Afterwards, however, they hadn't spoken about it.

Damon had quickly resumed a businesslike demeanour as he'd filled in forms and organised their new hire car. When they stowed their luggage and drove away once more, he was a little paler and quieter than usual, but Bella didn't want to pry by asking questions, and she suspected he wasn't ready to be jollied into a better mood.

In time he might want to talk about his father, or he might not. It would be his choice.

As they drove on, with the road unfurling like a ribbon beneath their tyres and a long day of driving stretching ahead, Bella hunted for a safe conversation topic.

'It was interesting to see your reaction to the TV news last night,' she told him. 'The way you jumped on the phone—the dedicated foreign correspondent in action.'

'I've had my eye on that grub for years. I'd hate to see him slip through the net.'

'It must be very satisfying to know you can really make a difference through your work—when you can do something special—actually saving lives.'

Damon shrugged. 'I suppose so.'

'I know you do, Damon. What about that time all the people were stuck on a border crossing way up in the mountains? Winter was closing in and the messages weren't getting out to the aid agencies?'

His eyes widened with surprise. 'Okay. I admit that was a good outcome. It was also a good story and I happened to be the only correspondent up there.'

'How did that happen?'

'Good luck, or bad luck, depending which way you look at it. Our chopper had put down in bad weather, so I was waiting for it to clear. And there they were—hundreds of people trapped, and no one knowing about it.'

He shot Bella a searching glance. 'That happened two years ago.'

'Yes, I remember.'

His eyes widened. 'I didn't know you were so well-informed about world events—or my career.'

'You're not making sexist assumptions, are you, Damon? I read more than fashion magazines and romance novels. I'm also concerned and interested in what's happening in the rest of the world.'

'Of course you are. I should have known that. You were always keen to find out about the world beyond Willara even when you were a kid.'

His smile sent warmth swirling all the way through her.

As they drove on she sighed. 'I'm afraid I don't do enough to help the people in other countries.'

'You've been helping your parents,' Damon reminded her.

'That's true. And I know charity starts with your family, but—' Bella stopped in mid-sentence as she saw the sudden tightness in Damon's jaw.

He was tense because she'd raised the F word. Family.

It occurred to her that they'd been travelling in opposite directions for the past ten years. Damon had set clear career goals that had taken him farther and farther away from his family. She'd stayed in Brisbane, which was reasonably close to Willara, and she'd become totally involved in helping her parents.

Now they were both at an uncomfortable crossroads.

Damon had come home, but he still wanted to avoid his past. She, on the other hand, was more or less freed of her family responsibilities, and in a position to travel and do whatever she liked, but she had no focus, no goal.

Not that there was anything to be gained by pointing this out to Damon.

Ahead of them, she saw the police station where they'd been detained. At least that ordeal was behind them.

Wanting to throw off their sombre mood, she said, 'We should call out good morning to our friend the constable.'

Damon grinned. 'I like the way this girl thinks. Yeah, why don't we give him a wave?'

His face had brightened in a flash and she saw the

naughty-boy smile she remembered so well, and, yes, there was a tad of defiance as he lowered his car window.

Bella let her window down, too. Already they were passing the neat little police building, and together they waved wildly and let out whoops and loud cheers.

There was no sign that they'd been heard, but it felt good to let off steam. By the time they'd sped past, they were laughing like silly schoolkids.

They exchanged sheepish smiles.

'I feel a damn sight better after that,' Damon said.

'Me, too.' Bella's smile was broad. For a brief moment, the years had dropped away, and they'd been their old selves.

She took a deep breath, and looked with new appreciation at the sunny blue skies overhead, and at the grassy cattle plains stretching wide on either side of them, the road as straight as an arrow. She found herself thinking fondly of the fun they'd shared in their past, when they'd been full of life and adventure.

'Do you remember some of the crazy things we used to do? Remember the hose fights? Or the time we smuggled you in a red wig and a tracksuit into the back of the netball bus?'

Damon chuckled. 'I'll never forget the look on my mates' faces when I waved to them out of the back of that bus.'

A moment later, he said, 'What about that time our English class placed a real-estate ad in the *Willara Chronicle* and we almost sold the school?'

'Oh, heavens, yes.' Bella laughed again as she remembered. 'I still have a copy of that advertisement. Lot four, Stevenson Road, Willara. Plenty of room. Grand old bargain. And then…the principal's phone number.'

'It was an April Fool's joke.'

'Strangely, Mr Brady didn't see the joke. He stood your whole class up at assembly, and said that every one of you would be punished unless someone confessed. So, of course, you stepped up.'

'Did I?'

'You know you did.' Bella looked at him. 'You were always willing to take the blame.'

'Someone had to.' Damon gave another shrug, then he turned to her with a thoughtful smile. 'What I mainly remember about those days is kissing you.'

Oh, help. Coming out of the blue, his comment sent Bella's cheeks flaming. By sheer willpower, she managed to speak calmly. 'I thought we'd agreed not to talk about any of that?'

'Sorry, but you started reminiscing,' he said, still smiling.

Bella felt more like crying.

Midmorning, she tried to phone their grandparents in Port Douglas, but there was no answer and no message bank, so no opportunity to make contact.

'They're probably out with their friends having a good time,' Damon suggested.

'I'm not sure about a good time if they were racing off to Port Douglas for an emergency.' Bella frowned. 'They might be at a hospital, or something grim like that.'

'Unless they used their emergency excuse as a cover.'

'Why would they need a cover?'

'They're *our* grandparents, after all. Perhaps they've taken off in search of adventure. Or romance.'

'Damon, be serious. Paddy and Violet are both in their eighties. You were terribly worried about Violet.'

'That's true,' he admitted. 'And I'll continue to worry about her until I hear that she's safe. But until we get to Port Douglas, there's not much we can do. So, it's not really worth dwelling on the negatives.'

Watching him, Bella saw the start of another smile. *What's this all about?* It was almost as if he was reverting back to the old Damon.

'So you haven't considered the possibility that Violet and Paddy have run away to elope?' he asked.

'No, I certainly haven't.'

'You don't think there's any chance of romance between them?'

'Damon, they're old friends. They've known each other for years. If they were going to have a romance, they wouldn't have waited till they were too old.'

'I'm sure they still feel young at heart.'

Bella rolled her eyes at this, but she couldn't help thinking about growing old and leaving things too late. She tried to imagine meeting Damon again when they were in their eighties and her heart gave a ridiculous leap, swiftly followed by a sweet, aching pang.

She sighed. It was useless to imagine romance with Damon in her old age, or at any age for that matter. She shouldn't even be thinking about it. If she'd fallen in love with anyone, it probably should have been Kent. But life was incredibly complicated and, unfortunately, emotions couldn't be organised on demand.

'You're very pensive.' Damon sent her a searching sideways glance. 'I'm sure they're okay.'

'Who?'

He chuckled. 'The people we've just been discussing. Our beloved grandparents, Paddy and Violet.'

'Oh, yes...of course.'

'So obviously you were thinking about something else?'

'Sort of. I started wondering about old age, and then I was thinking about—' Bella hesitated, but Damon was waiting for her answer.

'It doesn't matter,' she said. There was no point in telling him she'd been thinking about her close call with Kent. That was behind her now. She had to try to work out what she was doing with the rest of her life.

But not today.

They drove on. The sun climbed high and the miles slipped away, and after a while Bella turned on the radio and they listened to music.

They passed through lush green sugar-cane fields around Mackay, then stopped in Proserpine for lunch. Bella took a turn at driving, heading on through Bowen and around the outskirts of Townsville. From time to time, they talked—about the music on the radio, or about the scenery. They listened to a rather frustrating debate about global warming.

Whenever the news came on, Damon switched stations, much to Bella's surprise.

'I thought you'd be desperately interested in the news,' she said.

He shook his head. 'I get too intense about it, and I'm supposed to be on holidays.' He sent her a lazy smile. 'The world can do its worst for the next few days and someone else can report it.'

How interesting, she thought. *It really has been a day of changes.*

By late afternoon, they were approaching Cardwell, a sleepy beachside town nestled on the edge of a tropical bay with palm trees, a sunset and a gently lapping sea.

'I think we should stop and take a look here,' she said. 'It's lovely. We could have our dinner here.'

Damon was out of the car almost as soon as she pulled up. He let his head fall back, and drew in a deep lungful of the salty sea air. 'This is terrific. We should check out the accommodation here, and see if we can spend the night.'

Bella's mouth gaped in surprise. 'I thought you wanted to keep driving all night.'

'But it's so peaceful here.' He arched an eyebrow. 'Why would we want to rush past a lovely place like this?'

CHAPTER SEVEN

THE Coral Shore motel was very happy to offer them two separate rooms.

They dined on fish and chips, at a table on a white-painted veranda over which pink bougainvillea climbed. Their view was perfect—a tranquil, turquoise sea dotted with emerald-green islands and framed by palm trees.

After their meal, they strolled along the beach at the edge of the water, their bare feet pressing smooth, weathered lumps of coral into the damp sand.

The tropical air was tinged with purple from the last of the sunset. Their footsteps were accompanied by the soft lap-lapping of gentle waves, and an almost-full moon painted a silken, silvery path over the darkening waters.

It had been a hot day, but now a soft breeze blew, cooling Bella's skin and playing with flyaway strands of her hair, lifting the hem of her light cotton skirt.

Everything about this place was perfect, she decided.

For the past year and a half she'd been too busy racing between her work in Brisbane and her parents in Willara. She'd missed taking time for trips to the beach and now she found this setting idyllic and utterly magical, especially at the end of a rather surprising day.

Quite a different day from yesterday's drama with the police, but still unexpected...bringing this morning's emotional bombshell...then the exchange of happy, silly memories with Damon...

Most important of all, she'd rung Port Douglas again and had been able to get through to Paddy and Violet at last. Paddy told her that his old mate, Mick, had died two nights ago, and today he and Violet had been at the funeral and the wake.

Of course, Paddy was shocked to hear that Bella was in North Queensland. 'But, Bella, you're getting married on Saturday. I'm still hoping to be back in time for your wedding.'

Luckily, when she explained about the wedding, her grandfather took the news quite calmly.

'But does that mean you're travelling all this way on your own?'

'No, Damon's with me.'

'Damon Cavello?' This time there was no disguising his shock.

'He's worried about Violet. We were both worried, about the two of you, so we came together.'

Paddy chuckled then, surprised and delighted that anyone had come so far to rescue them.

It was just one more surprise in a surprising day. Bella thought. A day that had wrought an unmistakable change in Damon.

How could she have guessed that the man who'd driven all through the night would now want to wander along a tropical beach at dusk?

Mind you, this walk was causing a minor problem.

It wasn't easy to ignore Damon's breathtaking masculinity in this romantic setting. Moonlight glistened on his black hair and highlighted his dark throat against the whiteness of his open-necked shirt.

And when he turned to her his smile made her chest ache.

Bella was terribly afraid that, despite her best efforts, she hadn't gotten over this man, and she was going to be utterly miserable when he left her again. As he must. Now, as he stopped to pick up a smooth pink-and-white shell, she couldn't hold back a sigh.

He was smiling as he held the shell out to her. It was very pretty and delicate—perfect, without any chips or holes.

'It reminds me of you,' he said. 'It looks feminine and fragile, but it's actually quite tough and brave.'

To her dismay, her eyes were suddenly stinging. 'Thanks,' she said quickly. 'I might keep it, then.' Hastily, she slipped the shell into a pocket in her skirt.

She gave herself a stern lecture as they walked on. Damon had no idea how vulnerable she was right now. He had no idea she was battling with a head full of sweet memories and inappropriate longings. If he kept telling her such nice things she would break down and make a complete fool of herself.

They reached the end of the beach where a narrow channel separated the mainland from the steep, tree-studded spine of Hinchinbrook Island. Standing at the water's edge, they watched a small sailing boat make its way across the channel to an old wooden jetty on the island's shore.

Damon drew in a long, deep breath of cool, cleansing sea air and thought how beautiful it was here. So peaceful.

The sky was gradually growing darker, but it was perfectly clear, without a single cloud. Stars were appearing one by one, and, apart from the gentle lapping of waves at the sea's edge, the water was completely still.

He and Bella were the only people on the beach.

At that moment, it was quite possible to imagine they were the only two people on the planet.

Maybe I can relax now. Maybe now I can finally let go for a while.

He reached for Bella's hand and felt her sudden tension, saw the flare of surprise in her lovely green eyes. Almost immediately, her expression softened. Her cool, slim fingers linked with his and he was keenly aware of their skin touching, of their palms and fingers coming together, creating delicious centimetres of contact. He hadn't realised how he'd craved this simple gesture of comfort.

It was a perfect moment…his lovely Bella by a tropical sea… It was last night's fantasy come true. He lifted her fingers to his lips. Then, unable to resist anymore, he gathered her into his arms and kissed her.

CHAPTER EIGHT

ONE kiss was all it took.

One kiss fuelled by ten years of longing.

From the first trembling touch of their lips, Bella forgot everything except Damon.

In high school, he'd taught her how to kiss. Now, all these years later, he tasted exactly as she remembered. The texture of his lips, the pressure of his hands drawing her hard against him, the delicious stroke of his tongue...

Everything was utterly, instantly familiar.

But now she sensed a new level of expertise in him, an earthiness that drugged her senses and melted her inhibitions with staggering ease. From the moment they took the kiss deeper she could feel herself sliding helplessly into a hot, spiralling tunnel of need.

There was no point in trying to pretend she didn't want this. No time for discussions or debates.

They hurried up the beach and up the sandy stairs to their motel, stopping along the way for more kisses. Amazed, oh-my-God kisses. Long, lazy, sensuous kisses. Heady moments of joy and exciting rediscovery.

On the veranda outside her room, Bella couldn't restrain herself. While Damon dealt with the door key, she showered him with kisses on his jaw, on his ear lobe, his neck.

Inside, with the door safely shut, he reached for her and she fell into his arms with a glad, helpless cry. Their kisses turned greedy, hungry, ravenous. She threaded needy fingers in his hair and he kissed a burning trail along her collarbone.

'Bella,' he breathed against her ear. 'My green-eyed girl.'

'Don't say that. You'll make me cry.'

'Then I'll kiss you better.'

Playfully, he teased her ear lobe with the tip of his tongue and she was overtaken by a desperate need to nibble-kiss the rough skin along his jaw.

His lips found her breast through the soft fabric of her shirt, and a soft moan broke from her. Fever flooded her veins, swirling and licking into every secret part of her.

A heartbeat later, they sank together onto the bed, breathless and shaking with wanting each other, kissing, nibbling, devouring…scrambling out of clothes. Desperately, ecstatically on fire…

Afterwards, they lay close together in the dark listening to the wind rustling the palm fronds outside and the gentle splash of the tropical sea.

Bella let out a deeply contented sigh. 'I have to admit I haven't been that desperate since I was seventeen.'

'And for that I'll be eternally grateful.'

She felt his smile against her shoulder, was emboldened to ask, 'So, is it terribly uncool if I tell you that you were amazing?'

Laughing, he drew her closer, dropped kisses on her

nose and chin. 'You're the epitome of cool, Bella *bellissima*. Don't ever change.'

Don't ever change...

But they had changed. They'd chosen different paths. She didn't want to think about that, didn't want anything to spoil this night. She needed to be able to keep this night as a precious, perfect memory. 'Do you remember how we wanted our first time to be perfect? Rose petals, soft music, candles...'

'You wanted those things. I was more worried about finding a pharmacist who didn't know my father.'

She smiled. 'I saw us as Romeo and Juliet.'

'We were almost as tragic.'

A beat later, she asked the question that burned in her. 'So, who was your first?'

'I can't remember.'

'Liar.'

It was a while before he responded. 'Okay. It was a girl at university.'

Of course... Bella had been ready for that. Even so, she swallowed the sudden ache in her throat.

'There's something I've been meaning to tell you,' she said, then hurried on before she lost her nerve. 'The year after you left, I almost followed you to Queensland University.'

As soon as she said this, she held her breath, shocked by her own audacity. Surely it was foolish to indulge in a heart-searching analysis of the past. But if she and Damon were ever going to have this kind of conversation, it should be now.

'I wondered if you might,' he said softly. 'What happened? Did you change your mind?'

'Yes. I didn't think I could bear to be there if you

didn't want me, and you'd made it so clear when you left Willara that it was all over between us.'

'Yes…' The word was released on a heavy sigh. 'I was trying to protect you.'

'What from?'

'Me.'

'Oh, Damon.'

'I had to, Bella. It was the hardest thing I've ever done. But you still had another year of school, and I had to…leave…'

He picked up her hand and began to massage her palm, kneading it gently but firmly. 'Brown nail polish. That's novel.'

It was such an obvious and clumsy change of subject that Bella almost protested, but she didn't want to do or say anything that might spoil the magic of this night.

'It's called Dark Mocha,' she told him. 'And it's supposed to be very sophisticated. Do you like it?'

'It's great. Very chocolate and sexy.'

Slowly, he massaged his way along each finger joint. It was surprisingly relaxing and Bella was almost beginning to feel drowsy when the kneading stopped abruptly. 'Was your first time with Kent?'

She snatched her hand away. 'No! What makes you think that?'

'Just a hunch.'

'Well, you're way off the mark.'

'Who, then?'

'No one you know. A guy I met on holidays at the Gold Coast. Very brief and very forgettable.'

This was greeted by silence but Bella fancied she could see Damon grinning in the darkness.

His grin would probably be even wider if he knew

the truth about her dating life—that none of her relationships had lasted longer than a few months. Her boyfriends had been all okay, perfectly suitable guys, but before long she had always found fault with them, or lost interest. One fellow smiled too much. Another had small white hands. One was too smothering in his attention; another was too serious about life in general.

She'd never found a boyfriend who had everything on her wish list—someone fun and exciting and cool and sexy, with dark hair and grey eyes and strong capable hands.

It was pathetic to hang out for a replica of Damon. She knew that. She knew it was unrealistic, unfair and unwise. But she couldn't help it. Damon had left her with an unquenchable yearning.

And yet, he wasn't her One. He never could be.

Neither of them had the right to be possessive about other lovers. They weren't ever going to be a couple. They only had this one precious night and then Damon would be gone.

Reaching out, Bella touched his bicep, ran her fingers over the smooth, hard muscle until she found the elongated dimple of puckered skin. 'I hate to think about this bullet slicing through you.'

'It wasn't a bad wound.'

'But what if it had been here?' She pressed her hand over his heart and felt the drumming speed up beneath her palm.

'You worry too much.'

'I do. That's very true.'

'You never used to be a worrier.'

'Maybe I didn't have things to worry about.'

He rolled towards her, draped a possessive arm over

her hip. 'You're not going to add me to your worry list, are you?'

'Are we talking about when you go back to your life of war-torn strife and disaster?'

'Yes.'

She couldn't answer at first, had to wait for the ripples of panic to die down. 'No, I won't worry, Damon. I'm sure you'll stay safe. Only the good die young.'

He pressed a kiss to her forehead, let his hand glide over the sweet dip and curve of her hip. He kept the movement languid, but inside he felt the uneasy stirring of his conscience.

Taking Bella to bed was both the best and the least sensible move he'd ever made. In the end, he'd had little choice. From the moment she'd climbed into the sports car with him, he'd been battling with ten years' worth of loss. Then today they'd become so close. She had no idea how much she'd helped him, just by being there. Being Bella.

His Bella. Ever since he'd left her, she'd remained his emotional touchstone. So many times, when he'd found himself growing too jaded or cynical about the chaos he'd witnessed, he'd only had to think of this girl's unquestioning loyalty and the way she'd made him feel. Each time he'd remembered her faith in him, his ability to care about his fellow human beings had revived.

This mysterious bond that had survived between them was incredibly special. More than chemistry, beyond friendship and ordinary closeness.

He wouldn't let himself think about love, of course. He'd seen through that rose-coloured dream long ago. And perhaps he could thank his father for an inherited ability to keep his heart safely under lock and key.

But he did have to worry about Bella. He'd been so determined that he wouldn't mess her around, wouldn't hurt her. Now, he could only hope that she'd accepted this night for what it was—a one-off chance to reclaim the lost dreams of their youth, and then to let them go.

This was an opportunity to gain closure at last.

'Damon?' Her voice reached him softly through the darkness. 'Are you going to sleep?'

'Not a chance.'

'That's a relief. I was starting to worry again.' She snuggled closer, bringing with her the scent of wild-flowers, and he felt the smooth arch of her foot slide over his leg.

A moment later, she wriggled her toes against the inside of his thigh.

'Minx,' he growled as he pulled her to him.

'That I am,' she agreed. 'And I want to be pleasured.'

'Pleasured?' he repeated, amused.

'Mmm…' She stretched against him in a slow, silky slide of pink and white lusciousness.

He brushed the lightest of kisses over her skin, the first of the many he planned to give her, and he told himself one more time that this sad-happy pain in his heart could not, *dared* not be love.

The telephone woke them.

Bella dragged herself from her cosy haven against Damon's shoulder, brushed her hair from her eyes and groped for her mobile on the nightstand beside her. She blinked at the pale daylight filtering through the bamboo blinds and onto their bed. 'Hello.'

'Bella, it's Paddy. Sorry if I've woken you.'

'That's okay, Paddy.' She saw Damon's eyes snap open. 'Is everything all right with you?'

'Violet and I are fine. But listen, I'm ringing to tell you not to come any farther north.'

'Really? But we're almost there. We're already in Cardwell.'

'I know and you should turn around now.'

'Paddy, why?' She shook her head at Damon and sent him an eyebrow-raised look of helpless frustration.

He sat up, frowning. 'What's going on?'

'I'm not sure.' Mildly alarmed, Bella spoke into the phone. 'You can't send us home now, Paddy. Not when we've come so far. We've been worried about you.' She tried to think of reasons for her grandfather's unexpected blocking tactics. Was he going a bit dotty?

'So you haven't heard about the weather?' he said.

'No.' Bella couldn't remember the last time she'd listened to a weather report. It must have been at least a week ago. She'd been too busy dealing with wedding preparations, then calling the wedding off and *then* the emotional roller-coaster with Damon. Weather had been the very last thing on her mind.

Yesterday, they'd had the car radio on, but Damon had switched stations whenever the news came on. 'What's happening with the weather?' An unpleasant thought struck. 'Not a cyclone?'

'Yes, and it's heading this way.'

'To Port Douglas?'

'Looks like it.'

'Gosh. How close is it?'

'It's due to cross the coast sometime tonight.'

'Paddy, that's awful. What do you want us to do, then? Wait for you here? Meet you in Cairns?'

Beside her, Damon rolled out of bed and went to the window. With a tweak of the bamboo blind he showed her a cropped view outside of a grey sky, thick with low clouds.

'We're going to stay put,' Paddy told her. 'We can't desert Jessie.'

'Who's Jessie?'

'Mick's widow.'

'Oh, yes, I see.' Bella rubbed at her temple. This was all a bit much for so early in the morning. But she could imagine Paddy's predicament. A newly grieving widow would be in no state to face a cyclone alone.

'Jessie's son is a busy doctor and he flew back to Perth straight after the funeral,' Paddy explained. 'And the low only turned into a cyclone early this morning. She's all on her own. We've promised we'll stay.'

Bella nodded. 'I understand, and I'm sure she's very grateful to have you there. But if there is a cyclone, there's all the more reason why we should be there, too. We wouldn't want to impose on Jessie at such a sad time, but we could help to check that her house is safe.'

'Well, yes, that could be helpful.'

'Are there pot plants and bins and gardening tools that could get blown about?'

'Yes. I must admit we haven't thought about that. After living at Greenacres, we've become rather spoiled.'

'Don't worry. I could take care of it easily. And what about the roof and the windows? Damon could check those for Jessie.'

At this, Damon turned from the window and sent her a thumbs-up.

'You've got a point, love,' Paddy admitted. 'We probably could do with a hand.'

'I'm sure you could, so why don't you look after buying in supplies, and leave the heavy lifting for us? We'll be on the road as soon as we can. Should be there around lunch time.'

'Bella, that's kind of you. Now drive carefully, won't you?'

'We will, I promise. Just remember, don't try to do too much before we get there.'

As Bella finished the call she sank against the pillows, let out her breath with a whoosh. 'A cyclone.' She sent Damon a rueful smile. 'Who would have thought?'

'I suppose a cyclone's always on the cards if you're in the tropics in summer.'

'That's true, but it's still a bit early for the wet season. Gosh, what rotten luck.'

Pulling the sheet over her, she closed her eyes and nestled back into the pillow. 'I was looking forward to a leisurely sleep in, followed by a leisurely breakfast in bed.'

*Accompanied by leisurely lovemaking...*she added silently.

When Damon didn't respond, she opened one eye and saw that he was busy with his mobile phone.

'You're not turning into a journalist, are you, Damon? Getting first dibs on covering the cyclone?'

He smiled. 'It's tempting, but no. I'm checking the weather bureau on the internet. They have good cyclone tracking maps.'

A minute or two later he'd found what he wanted. 'Right. It's not a huge storm, but bad enough, and it's due to cross the coast between Port Douglas and Cairns some time around midnight.'

'If we're going to be any help, I guess we'd better get cracking, then.'

''Fraid so.'

'What a pity.' Her lower lip drooped as she contemplated the last pleasurable hour they might have shared.

Leaning over her, Damon nuzzled her ear. 'We could always save time by showering together.'

It wasn't a bad compromise.

'Are you heading north?' the young woman in Reception asked as they turned in their keys. 'You know there's a cyclone coming?'

'Yes, we've heard. Thanks, but we'll be okay,' Damon assured her. 'We have family in Port Douglas.'

The woman smiled back at him, her expression a mixture of coyness and curiosity. 'Most tourists are turning around, but I'm sure you know what you're doing, sir.' As she waved them off her smile was shrewd. 'I hope your rooms were comfortable.'

'Very comfortable, thanks,' Bella responded sweetly. She suspected that the other woman already knew they'd only used one of the rooms they'd paid for.

On the highway again, they drove through countryside that was noticeably tropical and lush. A fertile coastal plain, covered by farms of bananas, lychees, mangoes and sugar cane, was set against a majestic backdrop of rainforest-clad mountains with peaks wreathed in soft, cloudy mist.

It was almost like entering another country, Bella thought, and she might have enjoyed the scenery if she hadn't been so preoccupied with thinking about the night she'd just shared with Damon.

Last night had been...

Oh, God, her throat ached with dammed tears just thinking about how perfect it had been. From the moment they'd kissed on the beach there'd been no doubt, no question. She and Damon had both known that they were meant to have this—this one perfect night.

It was almost as if they'd slipped into a parallel universe where they could fulfil their true destiny, to live the life of their most secret desires and heartfelt dreams. One beautiful, passionate, glorious and tender night.

At least, Bella assumed one night was all she could hope for. Last night, she'd been happy to forego a where-is-this-taking-us conversation, but with the arrival of a new day questions were lining up in her head and she needed to talk.

News of the cyclone and their scramble to get on the road again hadn't given them any chance to talk. But now she knew it was time to negotiate her way down from the clouds.

But how did a girl start this kind of conversation?

She had no idea how Damon felt about their relationship now. Men, she knew, were notoriously reluctant to analyse their sexual encounters too deeply.

But as they drove through Tully and then on towards Innisfail, she knew she needed to *talk or burst*.

She was just about to broach the tricky topic when Damon turned on the car radio. 'Should be just about time for the latest weather report,' he said.

It gave more or less the same information they'd found on the internet. The cyclone was heading towards the coast and would cross during the night. It was a category two, but would probably intensify. As five was the highest category, it wasn't terrifying news, but any kind of cyclone caused damage.

'At least the cyclone more or less justifies our coming all this way,' Bella said. 'Paddy and Violet have obviously been coping very well, but I'm quite sure we can be helpful this afternoon. It's really important to be well prepared for a cyclone.'

'Have you ever been through one?'

'No,' she admitted. 'Have you?'

'A couple. I covered the aftermath of a very nasty one in Bangladesh.'

'I hope this one doesn't intensify.'

Bella had never been to Port Douglas or Cairns, but she knew both places had a reputation for their beauty and were very popular with tourists. She hated to think of them being destroyed. 'Let's hope the weather bureau's right. I don't think I could bear a natural disaster on top of everything else that's happened this week.'

'You're worrying again,' Damon warned her.

She managed a small smile. 'Okay. I've stopped.'

Then, like a swimmer plunging into cold water, she broached the subject that was even more important to her. 'Do you mind if we talk...about...us?'

At least Damon didn't flinch, but she saw his Adam's apple slide up and down in his throat. 'Sure. Are you worrying about us, as well?'

'Not really, but I'd like to get things clear. To make sure we're both on the same page.'

'What about?'

'Last night.'

Bella shot a wary glance Damon's way, but he kept his eyes straight ahead.

She took a deep breath. 'I mean, it was something that more or less had to happen, wasn't it? For all kinds of reasons.' Nervously, she chewed at her lip, then hurried on before her courage deserted her. 'I think we needed last night, because we were cheated out of it when we were young. So I guess it was more or less closure on the past.'

'I guess.'

Bella waited for him to say more, but he didn't.

This man, who was so eloquent on a television screen, had summed up the most beautiful night of her life with *I guess.*

Tense as a violin string, Bella tried again. 'There's no point in getting involved, is there? You'll be leaving again soon.'

'Not for another week or so.'

'What are you saying? That we could continue sleeping together for a week or so?' She couldn't hold back a cold little laugh. 'And then what? We get together again in another ten years? Or when you come home for weddings or funerals?'

Damon didn't reply, and she saw his mouth flatten into grimness.

Eventually, he said quietly, 'So, what are *you* saying? That it's probably best if we don't even consider a repeat of last night?'

A wave of utter despair swept over her. This wasn't what she wanted at all, but surely it was the only sensible option. 'If we continue the way we were last night, we'll—'

She had to calm the rising panic inside her before she could go on. 'Don't you agree it would be a mistake for us to get in too deep?'

Damon took his time answering. She could see obvious signs of tension in his jaw and in the way his hands gripped the steering wheel. But the realisation that he was finding this difficult didn't cheer her. She knew that inevitably he planned to walk away from her again.

After an age, he said wearily, 'I'm sure you're right.'

So expected, so sensible, but so *not* what she'd wanted to hear.

Terrified that she might cry, Bella pressed three fingers against her lips. She mustn't cry, mustn't spoil the special memories of last night by making a scene now.

She'd known from the moment she got into his car in Willara that she was taking a huge risk with her heart. Now, she had to accept the reality. She would probably never get over Damon. He was always going to be a part of her, a bittersweet scar that she carried for the rest of her life.

If she was honest, she had to admit that she'd more or less kept her life on hold since Damon left her the first time. Her work and her relationships had never been vitally important to her. She'd been filling in time. Stupidly hoping.

She'd never really let him go.

Now she had to face painful facts. Her only hope of long-term happiness was to put this lovely night behind her. She had to learn to live without Damon Cavello.

To add to her misery, these unhappy thoughts were accompanied by the first drops of rain.

The rain grew heavier as they drove on through Innisfail and Cairns and then on to Port Douglas. At times the windscreen wipers struggled to provide a clear view of the narrow, two-lane highway that skimmed the pretty coastline where the steep rainforest-clad mountains came right to the edge of the sea. Fortunately, most of the traffic was heading south.

In Port Douglas they found Jessie's white painted bungalow one block back from the beach. Its windows were already crisscrossed with safety tape, and Paddy and Violet were waiting in the doorway. When Bella and Damon dashed through the rain they were greeted with open arms.

'What sweethearts you are!' Violet exclaimed. 'I can't believe you've come all this way simply because you were worried about us.' She was smiling through her tears as she hugged them.

Delicate as a bird, she clung to Damon's arm, and as they went into the house she kept patting him, as if she was worried he might suddenly vanish into thin air.

Bella knew exactly how she felt.

Jessie was a sweet-faced, plump woman with a riot of curly white hair. Her face, not surprisingly, showed signs of strain, but she seemed genuinely pleased to see them.

'I hope you don't mind, but I've made a list of things I'd like you to check for me,' she said shyly, once the initial introductions and expressions of sympathy had been exchanged.

'That's perfect,' Damon said, scanning the list. 'I'm only too happy to help.'

But before he could start Jessie insisted they sit down to the delicious asparagus quiche and salad she'd prepared.

After that, it was time to get busy. While Damon, wearing one of Jessie's husband's sailing jackets, braved the rain to check the roof, guttering, windows and doors,

Bella tidied the garden. Anything that might become an airborne missile in gale-force winds—pot plants, gardening tools, a broken trellis and garbage bins—all went into the garage.

Jessie and Violet had shopped and they'd stocked up on batteries for torches and tinned food that would be easy to heat on a gas ring if they lost power during the storm. Bella also hunted in Jessie's storage shed and found a gas light and an ice box.

With these things assembled, and the yard clear, she took a mug of coffee out to Damon. She found him boarding up a window.

'You probably think we'd forgotten about you out here,' she said, ducking to join him under an eave out of the rain.

'Thanks,' he said as he took the steaming mug. 'This will hit the spot.'

Raindrops glistened in his dark hair and his skin glowed from his exertions. The impulse to lean in and kiss him was enormous. Remembering her new resolution, Bella restrained herself.

She turned her attention to the neatly boarded set of windows. 'I didn't know you were a handyman.'

'I'm not, but I can manage to bang in a nail.' He gave the window a push. It didn't budge. 'I'm glad we were here in time to do this. Some of these casements would have blown out in a high wind.'

Looking around at the bright profusion of hibiscus and heliconias in Jessie's garden, Bella hoped the gale wouldn't be too fierce. It was awful to think this lovingly tended backyard might be a tangled mess by the morning.

'What's the latest on the weather?' Damon asked.

'Much the same. Do you have much more to do?'

'Two more windows here and a down pipe to clear at the front. How's everyone else?'

'We're pretty organised now, although Jessie's worried about where we're going to sleep.' Bella deliberately avoided meeting Damon's eyes as she said this. 'She doesn't have any spare beds, and I was about to tell her we'd go to a motel. But then I thought we should probably stay here tonight, in case there's any drama. Do you agree?'

'Absolutely.'

'I told Jessie we'll be fine in the lounge room. One on the sofa and one on the floor.'

Over the rim of his coffee mug, Damon's grey eyes held the ghost of a smile. 'I hope she was reassured.'

'I think so.' A sudden gust of wind almost caught Bella off balance. 'Damon, you'll come inside if things start flying about, won't you?'

'Of course. I won't take any risks today.' But as he looked about him at the wild sky and the thrashing foliage his expression was more excited than careful.

'You like this, don't you?' Bella observed. 'You love the hint of danger in the air.'

'I don't mind being out in the elements. It reminds me of sailing.'

She thought about the many times she'd seen him on TV reporting against a background of danger and chaos. 'I guess you're an adrenalin junkie.'

'Perhaps I am.' With a smile, he leaned towards her. 'So why don't you give me a kiss?'

It was so unexpected Bella forgot to object. 'Why?' she asked lamely. 'Because kissing is dangerous?'

'Exactly.'

She should have said no, should have taken a step back. She should have taken *several* steps back.

But she was still under the spell of last night's enchantment, and every cell in her body was already clamouring for the first touch of his lips.

Perhaps she was addicted, too? Damon was dangerous, and yet she found him almost impossible to give up. Right now, she really, really needed his kiss.

And what a lovely, warm, coffee-flavoured kiss it was. Friendly and non-threatening, and yet unmistakably staking a claim. Bella was just a little dizzy when he released her.

But almost immediately she regretted her weakness. 'That wasn't wise,' she told him primly.

'You, of all people, must know I've never claimed to be wise.' As he handed her the empty mug, however, his eyes flashed a silent apology.

In the kitchen, Bella found Violet and Jessie preparing ingredients for a casserole. She unearthed a knife and joined them, chopping leeks and carrots while Violet tied herbs into a *bouquet garni* and Jessie browned meat at the stove.

Rain beat against the now boarded-up windows and the kitchen was dark enough to have an electric light on, giving the room a cosy, companionable atmosphere. The radio was playing softly in the corner and a marmalade cat was supervising their endeavours from a position of comfort on a cushion-lined cane chair.

Bella enjoyed working with the two women, surrounded by the comforting aromas of fresh vegetables, herbs and simmering beef stock. She was reminded of contented evenings in their farmhouse kitchen at Blue Gums, helping her mother to prepare dinner.

A renewed feeling of calm began to settle over her, and when Jessie left the room, and Violet enquired, ever so discreetly, about the wedding's cancellation, Bella was able to explain the complicated but delicate situation with surprising serenity and ease.

'You've almost convinced me,' Violet said when Bella reached the end of her story. 'But there is something still bothering you, isn't there, dear?'

Violet's dark, intelligent gaze was so serious and penetrating, Bella was forced to look down. 'I'm totally relaxed about the break-up with Kent.'

'I see,' Violet said gently. 'So I can only assume that my grandson is the cause of your current worries.'

Although Bella blushed, she found it almost a relief to have her private pain exposed, especially by Violet who understood Damon better than anyone. 'I'll get over it,' she said.

Violet sighed. 'I sincerely hope you will.' With a bony arm around Bella's shoulders, she leaned closer. 'But I *was* hoping he'd come to his senses at last.'

CHAPTER NINE

As the afternoon wore on the weather grew wilder. Scuds of rain dashed against the kitchen window, and wind gusts made the trees thrash about wildly. When Bella peered out past the gaps in the window boards, she saw palm trees bending so low they looked as though they might snap.

'We'll lose a few tree branches tonight,' Jessie remarked with stoic resignation. 'All I ask is that the roof stays on.'

Bella's heart went out to her. She knew how utterly wretched with grief Jessie must be, yet the poor woman had to deal with a storm, as well, and a houseful of people. But going through the cyclone on her own would have been horrendous. At least she now had willing helpers who were younger and stronger.

Paddy kept an eye on the weather reports, popping into the kitchen every so often to report updates. The eye of the cyclone was heading a little farther to the south, which was really good news.

'If you have to be anywhere near a cyclone, it's better to be north of it,' he told them. 'Looks like we might be spared the worst, but it's still going to be a rough night.'

The casserole was in the oven by the time Damon

finished outside. The wind sent the door slamming behind him. He hung his wet coat in the laundry, then went to have a shower, emerging in jeans, but without a shirt and smelling wonderfully, temptingly clean.

Bella couldn't help staring… When he bent to rummage in his duffle bag for a clean T-shirt she had to take several deep breaths as she watched the play of muscles in his back.

'And now, I guess we just wait for the worst,' she said.

Right on cue the lights went out.

They lit the assembled candles and gas lamp. Damon, armed with Jessie's oven gloves, shifted the casserole to the gas ring, and Paddy turned the radio off at the wall and switched it over to battery power. Outside, the winds revved up several notches, roaring and howling like the advance guard of a menacing invader.

Thanks to Damon's efforts, however, the windows didn't rattle and the roof didn't leak. There was no screech of ripping iron. The inside of the house was bathed in the gentle yellow glow of the gas lamp and everyone felt quite snug and safe.

Over and over Jessie told them how grateful she was for their company, but when a particularly nasty wind gust caused a loud thump against the side of the house she came close to tears.

Paddy poured her a glass of sherry and Violet suggested a board game.

Within minutes, everyone was gathered around the dining table in the light of the gas lamp, all happy to be absorbed in the game, rather than the tempest raging outside.

The evening slipped into night, and the fury of the storm became harder to ignore. To everyone's relief, however, the inside of the house retained its aura of calm. The casserole proved to be quite delicious, despite being finished off on the gas ring. They ate by candlelight, and opened a bottle of wine.

'As a morale booster,' Paddy said, freeing the cork from a fine red.

Dinner conversation was deliberately pleasant and relaxed, even when Paddy talked about his friendship with Jessie's husband.

'Mick and I were mates in Korea,' he explained to Bella and Damon. 'We used to get up to all kinds of mischief. Then I was wounded—shot in the leg, just at dusk. I was in a forward position on my own when our platoon was ordered to retreat. Good old Mick came back during the night and pulled me out.'

'Wow. A true hero,' Bella said softly. 'No wonder you've stayed close.'

'Paddy was best man at our wedding,' Jessie added with a gentle smile. 'And Mick was best man when Paddy married your grandmother, Bella.'

They might have become a little sentimental then, thinking about the past, but there was a sudden, frightening crash outside. Damon went to the door to check and reported that a tree on the footpath had come down onto the road.

As if to distract them, he flashed a twinkling smile and introduced a new topic of conversation. 'Has Bella told you about our little drama with the police on the way up here?'

This was greeted by exclamations of surprise.

'I take it this wasn't just a speeding ticket,' said Violet.

Taking turns, Bella and Damon related their experience in the lockup, making light of it, of course, and eventually eliciting smiles and laughter from their listeners. This led to more tales from Damon about his adventures overseas, and for a while, at least, the cyclone was almost forgotten.

Violet had made a dessert, which Damon greeted with a whoop of boyish delight.

'Mango trifle. My all-time favourite,' he explained for the others' benefit. 'I still dream about it on a regular basis.'

'If you came home more often,' Violet commented, 'you wouldn't have to dream about the things you've missed.'

Across the table, Damon's eyes met Bella's, and she knew he was remembering the unhappy conclusion they'd reached this morning. But Violet was watching them, her dark eyes sharp and aware, and Bella quickly dropped her gaze to her plate.

After dinner, while the 'elders,' as Bella had named them, played cards, she and Damon heated water on the gas ring, and dealt with the washing up.

Every so often, Damon went to the front door and stuck his head outside. The roar of the wind was astonishing, like a freight train rushing past, but as the whole of Port Douglas was in darkness there was very little to see, apart from the glimpses he could catch in the beam of his torch.

'The rain's horizontal,' he reported.

'Ooh, let me see.' Bella rushed to join him in the

doorway, their bodies brushing. She held her breath, reminded herself to be more careful.

Jessie found rain seeping in under one or two windows, bringing with it tiny pieces of leaves, so with Bella's help she shoved old towels into the cracks. Damon made hot chocolate for everyone and they played another board game. At ten o'clock, Paddy, Violet and Jessie opted to retire to bed.

'Might as well try to get some sleep,' Violet said. 'Although it's going to be a challenge with that racket outside.'

Jessie brought Bella a pile of pillows and quilts. 'Are you sure you'll be all right in the lounge room?' she asked one more time.

'We'll be as snug as bugs in rugs,' Damon assured her.

'Yes, please don't worry,' Bella reinforced. 'Damon can sleep anywhere. Didn't you know? He just gathers up a pile of rocks in the Sinai Desert and sleeps like a baby.'

Jessie laughed at that and hugged them. 'You're darlings, both of you, and thank you so much for your help today. I can see why Paddy and Violet are so proud of you. We certainly couldn't have managed on our own.'

'Well, I do feel that our trip up the highway was worthwhile now,' Bella said when they were alone once again and sitting in the soft glow of the lamplight while the wind raged and battled outside.

Actually...Bella was sitting rather stiffly on the edge of the lounge, while Damon sprawled in an armchair.

He wondered if she was tense because she was trying, as he was, to cancel out memories of their previous night…the tropical beach…the moon…and the bliss of their shared bed…

'Sleepy?' he asked her now, sending her a deliberately lazy smile.

'I know I should be exhausted, but I think I'm too keyed up to sleep.'

'Board games can do that to you.'

She laughed. 'Board games *and* a cyclone.'

Board games, a cyclone and being alone with each other for yet another night when we've agreed it isn't wise.

Already, he'd made the unwise move of kissing her again today. Now, he was hunting for a safe, non-threatening, non-personal subject for them to talk about.

It was going to be a long night.

'Would you like another drink?' Bella asked hospitably. 'I don't think we finished that bottle.'

Damon shook his head. 'Probably not a good idea. We haven't seen the worst of this storm yet, and we should keep our wits about us.'

As if to underline his comment, the rain hammered against the house and from somewhere down the street came the screech of ripping iron.

Bella flinched at the noise, then sent him a theatrical, raised-eyebrow look of surprise. 'I thought you foreign-correspondent types were all supposed to be heavy drinkers.'

'You're thinking of the glory days of the old-style foreign correspondents. Sadly, they're long gone.'

'What are you implying, Damon? That modern journalists are boring and pure?'

'As the driven snow,' he said dryly.

But then, aware that she was as keen as he was to talk

about anything but their too-brief relationship, he went on more seriously, 'The thing is, foreign correspondents are not just gathering news these days. We're dealing with all the new technology, as well. A lot of overseas bureaus have closed down, so we're editing our own work on our laptops. Then we have to network with emails, websites, et cetera. I rarely have a cameraman with me. More often than not, I'm using a hand-held webcam. You can't afford to lose concentration.'

'It does sound rather demanding.'

'It's certainly not as glamorous as most people imagine. And in many countries there's a total ban on alcohol. In fact,' he added with a wry grin, 'I downed more grog at Kent's bucks' party than I have in years.'

'I'm sure you weren't the only one who got stuck into it that night.'

Although Bella spoke lightly, an awkward silence fell.

'Perhaps I should check how the others are.' Bella, already on her feet, disappeared down the hallway to the bedrooms.

Before long she was back. 'All good. No one's asleep, but they're not too scared. Paddy's listening to the radio. He said the cyclone's crossing the coast south of us now between Cairns and Innisfail.'

She sank onto the sofa again, this time curling her slim legs beneath her, and Damon thought, as he had so many times in the past few days, how lovely she was.

Lovely, and yet, since this morning's unsettling conversation, she'd also looked fragile, as if she were holding herself together with string and a paper clip.

He felt wretched, too. For one night she'd been his Bella, as reckless and wild as she was responsive and loving. For one night they had opened a window on a dream and, like all dreams, it was as fleeting and impossible to hold onto as a soap bubble.

Damon had been left with an aching desire for Bella that was stronger than it had ever been.

But, unfortunately, she'd asked the right questions this morning.

What was the point of becoming more deeply involved? He had no intention of settling down to a desk job in an Australian newsroom. He would find it stifling, to say the least.

As if she guessed the direction of his thoughts, Bella gave a huff of impatience, and was on her feet again, frowning and tense as she sorted through the pile of bedding Jessie had left for them. No doubt she was unhappy with him for sitting here brooding when the dark and blustering night called for entertaining stories, distracting jokes and witty repartee.

'Do you prefer firm or soft?' she asked.

'I beg your pardon?'

She held up a pillow, prodding it in a businesslike fashion.

'Oh, I'll take whatever comes.'

'Here, catch.' She tossed him a plump, firmish pillow. 'You might like a quilt, as well.' She set one down on the carpet. 'You can use it as a mattress, and then wrap yourself up in it if it gets cold in the early hours.'

'I take it you're going to try to sleep?'

'I'm going to lie down, at any rate.'

'Would you like me to turn out the lamp?'

'Not yet, thanks.'

She rearranged pillows on the sofa and lay, curled on her side.

Damon stretched out on his back on the carpet, one arm crooked above his head, his legs crossed at the ankles.

'Comfy enough?' she asked.

'Exceptionally. How about you?'

'I'm fine, thanks.'

But before they could settle, there was a terrifying thump outside and a shocking, splintering crash.

'That was close,' Damon said. 'I'd better check.'

At the front door again, he braced against the force of the wind. He flashed his torch through the driving, slanting rain and saw, to his horror, that a tree had fallen onto the house across the road. The front corner of the house's roof had completely caved in.

Bella was beside him. 'Is it bad?'

'A tree on a neighbour's house.'

'Oh, no. I wonder if there's anybody in there. I'll go and ask Jessie if she knows them.'

But Jessie was already in the hallway behind them. She'd pulled a cardigan on over her nightdress and her eyes were wide with fright. 'Which house is it?' she asked querulously.

'Opposite and about two doors along.'

'The white weatherboard?'

'That's it,' said Damon. 'Is it occupied?'

'Yes. Oh, dear. They're a lovely young couple with a darling baby. Cassie and Michael Evans and little Jordan.'

Damon didn't hesitate. 'I'll go over to check, to make sure they're all right.'

Jessie shook her head at him. 'No. You can't go out now. Not in that wind.'

'Damon, you promised you wouldn't take risks,' Bella reminded him.

His impulse was to ignore them, and he might have done so if Paddy hadn't appeared at the moment.

'I just heard on the radio that the eye should be passing over us very soon,' he said. 'The winds will die down for a few minutes at least. You could go over there then, Damon.'

'OK. That's what I'll do.'

'And I'll come with you,' Bella announced.

He shook his head at her. 'Bella, don't be silly.'

'Why is it silly for me to do exactly what you're doing? If those poor people need help, two pairs of hands will be better than one.'

Not your hands, he wanted to yell. But he saw the defiant gleam in her eye. She was telling him firmly that, for once, she wasn't going to be left behind.

To his surprise, neither Paddy nor Jessie disagreed with her.

Five minutes later, as predicted, the wind died as if an unseen conductor had waved his baton. The sudden silence was eerie.

As Bella and Damon stepped outside the house they were surrounded by thick, impenetrable darkness.

In a torch's beam they saw a scene of distressing devastation. It was how Bella imagined that Armageddon might look—trees without limbs, lamp-posts leaning drunkenly, trailing wires onto the littered footpath. But they didn't have time to investigate too closely. At any minute, the winds would return even fiercer than before.

'Stay close to me,' Damon ordered. 'We have to keep

well away from those fallen power lines. Here, give me your hand.'

Although Bella was determined to be brave, she was very grateful for his warm, strong handclasp. Together, they made their way as quickly as possible, picking their way carefully between the fallen branches and piles of debris.

As they reached the neighbours' house, they could see the caved-in roof and a sickening hole gaping beneath the trunk of a huge Poinciana tree.

'Hello!' Damon yelled. 'Is anyone in there?'

Almost immediately a torch beam waved in a window. 'Yes, mate,' a male voice called back. 'We're here.'

'Are you okay? Is anyone hurt?'

'No, we're all fine, thanks. The tree missed us. We were in the bedroom at the back.'

'That's good news,' Damon called. 'So you don't need any help?'

'No, thanks. Not now. It'll be a different story in the morning.'

'Okay, we'll see you then.' Damon tugged on Bella's hand. 'Come on, the wind's already picking up. We'd better get back.'

He'd hardly said this before a roaring wind gust rushed at them so strongly it pushed Bella against Damon. He staggered sideways, losing hold of her hand as he fought to keep his balance.

Almost immediately, another ferocious wind gust, like a fist slamming into Bella's back, pushed her to her knees. A tree branch flew past her head, missing her by inches. To her shame she screamed. She couldn't help it. The force of the wind was incredible. Rain stung her face, and she could scarcely breathe, could barely see.

She felt Damon's hands beneath her armpits, hauling her to her feet. He flung both arms around her holding her tightly. Another piece of debris came flying out of the darkness.

Bella screamed again and Damon swore. He shone the torch across the road, where Jessie's house, on the far side of a wall of blinding, sheeting, horizontal rain, now looked a hundred, impossible miles away. As they watched a sheet of roofing iron skidded down the street. Bella imagined its sharp edge slicing into her and winced.

'There's a garden shed over here.' Damon flashed the torch a few feet to his right. 'Let's get in there. Here, link elbows. It's a stronger hold.'

Gripping each other tightly, they staggered to the shed. Bella fell against the door, puffing from fright and exertion. The door had a barrel vault, which was a bit rusty and hard to shift, but it wasn't locked, thank heavens.

Soon Damon had it free and they hurried inside and slammed the door behind them. At last. Safety.

'Are you okay, Bella?'

'Yes.'

He shone the light in her face, making her blink. 'Sorry.' Quickly, he shone the beam around the shed, re-vealing glimpses of gardening tools. A spade, a shovel, forks and a rake, dusty fishing nets on the walls, a lawn-mower and a wheelbarrow, stacks of flowerpots, tins of paint and folded tarpaulins. 'I'm afraid it's not quite as comfortable as Jessie's lounge-room floor.'

'It'll be fine for the moment.' Bella was happy to be anywhere that was dry and out of that terrible wind.

They took off their dripping raincoats and hung them over the lawnmower's handle.

'We should ring Paddy,' Bella said.

Before they'd left Jessie's house, they'd given Paddy her mobile phone so they could keep in touch.

Now Damon dug his phone out of his jeans pocket, and the light from its screen cast an eerie blue glow as he keyed in Bella's number.

'Damon!' Paddy shouted almost immediately. 'Where the hell are you?'

'We're still over the road. Tell Jessie her neighbours are okay, and we're sheltering in their garden shed. It's too hairy out there to try to come back. We'll wait till this wind stops.'

'Okay. Good idea. Whatever you do, stay safe.'

That dealt with, Damon hauled the painting tarpaulins into the small space in the middle of the shed to try to make a slightly more comfortable place for them to sit.

Reaching for Bella's hand, he shone the torch on the rough nest he'd made. 'These tarps are a bit smelly but they're better than sitting on bare concrete. Let me show you to your seat, madam.'

She laughed. 'Thank you, kind sir.'

'If you bunch it up you can make a bit of a cushion.'

'Yes, I'm quite comfortable, thanks.'

In the glow of the torch, he could see the pale gleam of her hair. She was sitting cross-legged and leaning back against a wooden crate. She sent him a brave little smile.

'Okay with you if I turn the torch off now?'

'Yes. Go ahead. Save the battery.'

They were plunged into darkness, while outside the raging storm continued.

Bella's voice reached him, warm and teasing. 'I knew if I stuck with you, I'd have another adventure.'

He grimaced in the darkness. 'Sure. First a police lockup, now the floor of a garden shed in the middle of a gale. Excitement and thrills guaranteed—although possibly not comfort.'

'At least no one's shooting at us.'

'Stick with me long enough, and you can have bullets, too.'

Bella didn't respond and Damon flinched as he realised what he'd said. *Stick with me long enough and you can have bullets...*

How thoughtless was that? Making a joke of the very thing that kept the two of them apart.

He closed his eyes and was immediately assailed by images of Bella—bravely sitting it out in the police lockup, of her working hard today, pitching in to help any way she could, of her walking along the beach at dusk, as alluring as a mermaid. The exquisite pleasure of taking her into his arms—*at last*—every luscious detail of her skin, her scent, her flattering hunger.

No wonder this particular girl had such a hold on his heart. Seeing her again should have loosened the old ties, but they'd drawn her closer. He had no idea what he was going to do about that.

'Damon?'

'Yes?'

'Have you ever asked yourself why you're always so eager to leap into dangerous situations? Have you ever wondered what triggered the urge in the first place, before it became a habit?'

'No, I haven't,' he said quickly, fighting a sudden flare of panic.

'So you pose all kinds of searching questions to all kinds of people all over the world, but you never ask them about yourself?'

She was right, of course. He made a point of *not* asking questions of himself.

And the reason was easy. He didn't want to know the answers.

'I've always hated to be bored,' he said. 'So my job's perfect. But I suppose a shrink would tell me that I was doing it to prove something to my father.'

'And to your mother perhaps?' Bella asked.

His mother?

Without warning, Damon's heart toppled from a huge height. Valiantly, he tried to ignore the pain. 'It doesn't matter what she thought.' She'd abandoned him and he preferred to forget about her. He'd worked hard to forget her.

But in the thick, musty darkness with the storm raging about them, he couldn't hold back the boyhood memories.

He saw his mother's gentle smile, and he felt the wonderful warmth of her hug. He could even smell her perfume, and he remembered being four years old with the chicken pox and feeling the soothing touch of her cool hands as she applied lotion to his skin.

He remembered her voice at bedtime, animated and lively as she read his favourite stories. He remembered how he'd adored her, how he'd always loved coming home from school. Their house had such a welcoming feel, and the smell of furniture polish and the flowers she arranged in vases, and the gingerbread she'd baked for afternoon tea.

Oh, God. He could never recall these sweet memories without being swamped by the agony of her desertion. Now he was racked, once again, by his devastating, ten-year-old bewilderment. By his father's despairing rage.

The pain of these memories had always been so terrible Damon had trained himself to keep them locked out. They were not on his emotional agenda.

But now, covering his face with his hands, he was determined that he must not break down again. Not in front of Bella. He couldn't bear it.

Beside him, he heard a soft sound, felt a stirring of the air. Then he heard Bella's whispered voice. 'I'm so sorry.'

She was kneeling beside him. 'Damon, I'm sorry. I shouldn't have thrown your mother into the conversation like that. I hope I haven't upset you.'

With a supreme effort of will, he conquered the emotions that were storming inside him as savagely as the wind and rain. 'Don't worry. It's okay. I'm okay.'

Through the darkness her fingers found his cheek. She ran a gentle caress along his jaw. 'You don't have to be the tough guy all the time, you know?'

'Yeah…I know.' He let out a long breath. Enough with the memories.

Reaching for her hand, he drew it to his mouth and pressed a kiss against her fingers. 'But you know there are advantages to playing it tough.'

'You think so?'

'Sure. The tough guy always gets the girl.'

He heard a tiny cry. 'Yes,' Bella said in a suddenly

squeaky voice. 'He gets her even when she tries to stay away.'

He reached for her in the darkness. His hand touched her hair, then her cheek and he discovered tears.

'Bella,' he murmured hoarsely as he tried to blot the damp trail of her tears with the pad of his thumb. 'I've given you a raw deal, haven't I?' He swallowed the burning brick in his throat. 'Brave girl.'

'Not so brave tonight.'

He might have drawn her to him then. Not to seduce, but to offer her comfort.

But she said, 'Damon, listen.'

He turned his attention to the storm outside.

'It's not roaring quite so loudly now,' Bella suggested.

'I think you're right. I'll take a look.' He found the torch and went to the door. 'It's not nearly as bad as it was before. We could probably make it back to Jessie's. Do you want to make a run for it?'

'We might as well.' She was already beside him, pulling on her raincoat.

Moments later, they were making their way back through the wind and the rain, holding hands as they dodged fallen debris.

It was probably the silence that woke Bella. At first she lay in a disoriented haze, slowly assimilating her surroundings. She was lying on the sofa in Jessie's lounge room and there was a dent in the pillow on the abandoned quilt on the floor where Damon had slept. She could smell freshly brewed coffee, coming, no doubt, from the kitchen.

Looking up, she saw pale glimmers of daylight slanting through the boards on the windows and, finally, she registered the silence. Not a whisper of wind or rain. Just the sound of a car starting up farther down the street.

The cyclone had passed.

Somewhat stiffly, she sat up, surprised that she'd slept so well. She'd been in such a state of emotional turmoil last night, she'd expected to toss and turn for hours. But in the end the incessant roar of the wind had worked like a lullaby and she'd slept like a baby.

Now, she heard voices in the kitchen and she jumped to her feet, ran her fingers through her messy hair.

Damon appeared in the kitchen doorway, dressed in jeans, but without a shirt. He was holding a mug. 'Ah, the princess wakes. I was bringing Your Highness a cup of coffee.'

Bella tried very hard to ignore his nicely muscled torso. She was sure he was more toned than most men who spent their days with a laptop and a camcorder. 'Am I the last one up?'

'No. Paddy and I have decided to let the girls sleep in.'

'That's nice.' She took the mug and sipped. The coffee was hot and not too milky. Just right. 'Is the electricity back on?'

Damon shook his head. 'I'd say it'll be days or even weeks before they can mend all powerlines.'

'Oh. That's rough for Jessie. What's it like outside?'

'Not a pretty sight.' He cocked a head towards the door. 'Come and see for yourself.'

Even though Bella had seen glimpses of the wreckage last night, she was shocked by the mess of tangled branches and shredded foliage that littered Jessie's once-pretty garden. Even the front porch was hidden under a carpet of sodden leaves and broken twigs.

A massive tree lay uprooted on the road, its exposed roots dangling, while from overhead broken powerlines hung. Worse, was the other tree that had smashed the neighbour's roof.

'I don't suppose Jessie's seen this,' Bella said.

'No. Paddy's talked her into having breakfast in bed.'

'Poor darling.'

'At least we're here to clean it up for her.'

Bella smiled at him. 'For someone who was determined to be a bad boy, you've grown up into a surprisingly good man.'

CHAPTER TEN

Bliss.

Bliss to soak away the mud and the garden grime. Bliss to ease her stiffening muscles, and to look forward to another peaceful, storm-free night in a proper bed.

After three days of hard work in Jessie's and her neighbours' gardens, Bella was exhausted and aching and grimy.

It had been rewarding work, of course. One of the good things about a disaster was that everyone in the neighbourhood pitched in to help each other. People who, normally, barely said hello had shared tools and gardening gear and lent a hand wherever it was needed. With no power, impromptu barbecues had been organised in backyards and food was shared.

And as Damon had found a motel with a good generator, they hadn't had to continue sleeping in Jessie's lounge room. Bella had been able to enjoy a hot bath each night. True bliss.

Not so blissful, in fact downright depressing, was the fact that she'd slept alone on each of these nights while Damon slept on the other side of a double-brick dividing wall.

Depressing or not, the arrangement had been Bella's

idea, and she knew it was totally sensible. Very soon Damon would be on the other side of the world. They'd be hemispheres apart, and she had to get used to the idea of living without him.

Actually, she had to return to her Damon-free life in less than twenty-four hours. In the morning she would be leaving Port Douglas. It was all arranged that she would fly to Brisbane while Damon drove back to Willara with Paddy and Violet.

It hadn't been an easy decision, but, again, it was sensible. Bella was not returning to Willara just yet. She had to start job hunting and she didn't want the others to have to make a rather long detour just to drive her to Brisbane.

Apart from that, she knew that spending more time on the road with Damon would only make the final farewell so much more difficult.

Besides, she was probably a coward, but she didn't think she could cope with Paddy and Violet's constant vigilance. She knew they were looking for clues to the true nature of her relationship with Damon.

If she'd been less conflicted about her feelings for him she might have coped. But, given her constant inner turmoil, this extra pressure would make the trip far too difficult.

But Bella's decision to fly meant that she didn't expect to see Damon again before he left Australia. So in the morning they would be saying goodbye.

Now, as she added soothing oils to her bathwater, she decided there was one good thing about being really, really tired. She didn't have the energy to panic.

That would come later.

* * *

Having insisted that the 'elders' enjoy a quiet dinner together on this final night, Bella and Damon found a place that served decent hamburgers. The picnic areas on the beachfront were still strewn with cyclone debris, so they took the burgers back to their motel rooms.

'My place or yours?' Damon asked as they pulled up outside.

Bella drew a sharp breath. She knew it was silly to be tense, but until now Damon hadn't set foot in her room, or she in his. 'Mine's probably not as tidy as yours, but I have good coffee,' she said, pleased that she sounded reasonably calm.

She wasn't quite so calm once they were inside her small room. The bed took up most of the space, and the tiny plastic dining table and two chairs were wedged in beside it.

'Choose any seat,' she said with a sharp little laugh.

They sat, rather awkwardly, on either side of the small table. But almost immediately Bella felt too hot, and she jumped up to turn down the air conditioning.

She was still hot and bothered. Damon, on the other hand, looked quite relaxed as he unwrapped his burger.

'Would you like a knife and fork?' she asked.

He recoiled in mock horror. 'The only way to eat a hamburger is with your hands.'

'And with bits of green stuff falling into your lap,' she said as she rescued shreds of lettuce that had already fallen from her bun.

Damon frowned, staring at her hands.

'What's the matter?' she asked.

'What happened to your fingernails?'

Bella looked down at her hands. 'I took off the polish. Why?'

'Let me see.'

Bemused, she set her hamburger down on its paper bag and spread her hands flat on the tabletop. 'My nails were in such a mess after all that garden work. I had to take the polish off and file them down. What's the big deal?'

With a strong fingertip he touched the nail on her forefinger. 'I've never seen them naked.'

Ridiculously, she felt a rush of heat. Somehow, she forced herself to be flippant. 'Well, there you go. A first. Maybe you can write about it in your next headline. Young woman exposes naked fingernails in North Queensland.'

He laughed, and let her hands go, sat back and regarded her with a look that made her insides tumble.

Oh, heavens. If only she hadn't made the mistake of falling in love again. Why did this have to be so hard?

If she were as widely travelled and worldly as Damon, she probably wouldn't have kept him at arm's length for these past two nights. And this wouldn't have to be goodbye. They would have made love every night and, after they parted they'd simply look forward to future reunions.

But that degree of sophistication was beyond Bella's reach. She might have worked in Brisbane for several years and started to think of herself as a city chick, but she was still a small-town girl at heart. A one-man girl.

Her city-girl values were like her nail polish—a veneer. Deep down, she wanted a man who could love her exclusively and forever. She'd spent all these years hopelessly in love with a bad boy when what she really wanted was a good guy. Someone permanent. Someone who wanted to hang out with her more than he wanted to run away.

Desperate to fight off these misery-making thoughts, Bella hastily deflected their conversation. 'I'm so glad we were able to help Jessie.'

'Yes. It was good to pitch in and help.'

'And tomorrow you'll definitely be helpful. I know Paddy and Violet are secretly relieved that you're driving back with them. I think they found the trip north much more tiring than they're prepared to admit.'

'But we'll miss your company, Bella.'

'Yes, well... You know why I'm not coming. I'm going back to Brisbane and that's out of your way.' Lifting her gaze to meet his piercing gaze, she said pointedly, 'Violet understands.'

'Yes, my grandmother's very perceptive.' Damon's eyes narrowed. 'But what, exactly, does she understand?'

'She's guessed about us. At least, she's sussed out that we—that we're still attracted. But she understands that it's all too complicated, and that if we continue in each other's company things will only become more complicated.'

'I see. So does this mean I'll be thoroughly grilled on the trip back?'

'Only if Violet thinks you deserve to be grilled.'

He looked as if he might comment on this, but Bella held up a hand. 'There's not much point talking about this, is there? We've made a decision, and we both know it's right.'

Then, before Damon could protest or she could weaken, she said, quickly, 'I'm actually very tired, and I'm sure you must be too, Damon.'

'Not particularly.' But he rose and rolled up the paper and crumbs from his hamburger and tossed them into the waste bin.

Standing in the middle of her room, empty handed, he said, 'I can't pretend I'm happy with the way things have worked out for us, but, God knows, I've caused you more than enough problems.'

Grim-faced, he crossed to the door. 'I'll leave you to enjoy your early night.'

Bella heard a faint thread of anger in his voice. Or was that regret? Whatever—she had no choice but to ignore it. 'Thanks,' she said, with a tight, unhappy smile.

'Good night, Bella.'

'Good night.'

She hated watching him leave, but she hated more that she couldn't trust herself to carry on a conversation tonight without becoming a blubbering mess.

The door closed quietly behind him, and she listened to his footsteps on the concrete path outside. She heard the key in his lock, heard the squeak of hinges as he opened his door, and then shut it again.

Heard the silence.

Oh, God.

This was the end. Damon would always be the love of her life and she was letting him go. How could she bear it?

Now she wanted to run after him, to knock and pound on his door, to beg him to come back, to stay with her for one last night.

Suddenly, she was shameless in her wanting.

Damon hurled the door key onto the small plastic table, a replica of the one in Bella's room, and he glared as he watched it slide across the table's surface and fall to the floor. The impulse to throw a few more things around the room was strong.

He was so mad with himself. So tormented. A mess inside—as chaotic as a war-torn, Third World country.

He wanted Bella.

But what had he to offer her besides an on-again and off-again affair? She deserved someone steadfast and rock solid who would always be there for her.

But whenever Damon imagined offering Bella his love—not physical love, but a heartfelt emotion that was true and deep and good—he was overcome by panicking powerlessness.

What did he know of love?

His father had always kept him at arm's length, and any happy memories of his mother's love always brought such a raft of sadness.

There'd been Violet, of course…

Violet's unstinting love had been the constant in his life. His rock. In the bad old days in Willara, Violet had always been there for him, and no matter how strained things were at home she'd been ready with a gentle smile, an understanding heart and a truckload of patience.

He'd never thought it strange that a teenage boy with a reputation for wildness should seek the company of his grandmother. Violet had never been a fussy, smothering grandmother. More often than not, he'd found her working in her beloved garden, and he would join her, helping to prune the heavier branches, or to dig out the tough weeds.

Whatever had happened…she'd always been *there*, ready to listen.

After he'd left Australia, Violet had never lost touch with him. Her letters and postcards had been his lifeline.

He knew her heart had broken along with his on the day his mother left, just as he knew she understood why his mother had run away. But she'd left when he was ten and it had been eight long years before he'd worked up the courage to ask that all-important question.

Just before he'd left Willara, he'd gone to her.

'Do you know why she left me?'

'Who, darling?'

'My mother.'

'Angela?' Violet's face had contorted. 'Damon, you know there was an accident. She was killed.'

'But she was leaving us.'

'She was leaving your father.'

That wasn't what his dad had told him. Jack Cavello, in his grief and rage, had shouted that it was all Damon's fault. His wickedness had driven his mother away.

His grandmother, however, had grabbed his arm with a wrinkled hand. 'Damon, Angela was planning to come back for you. She was going to fight to keep you. Surely you knew that?'

'No.' His mouth had pulled out of shape as he struggled not to cry. 'Why have you never told me that?'

'I thought you knew. You never asked.'

'I was afraid to.'

Hell.

Damon came to an abrupt halt as he ran smack into the truth.

Bella had hit the nail on the head when she'd asked about his mother on the night of the cyclone. While his conflict with his dad had been loud and blustering and obvious, his feelings for his mother had been buried, and, ultimately, much more painful.

A cold chill drenched him to the bone as he saw himself as he really was. Forever on the run.

Bella was mad with herself for sinking into a pit of desolation. She'd known all along that her journey with Damon wasn't going to end with romance and happy ever after. Foolishly, she'd still managed to trick herself into hoping for the impossible.

Now, she had no choice but to accept the blinding, obvious truth. She'd had nothing more than a brief, exciting fling with her high-school sweetheart and, like mature adults, she and Damon would now go their separate ways.

She was free to get on with the rest of her life.

With a sense of utter desolation, she went to the bathroom and washed her face, splashing cold water again and again until the red blotchiness caused by crying finally began to fade.

She looked at her reflection. Her eyes were still a little pink and when she tried to smile she looked strained. But perhaps signs of strain were forgivable given everything that had happened to her since she hopped into Damon's red sports car a week ago.

It was hard to believe it had only been a week. There'd been so much intense one-on-one time with Damon, and she felt as if she'd lived a lifetime of joy and despair.

And yet…just a mere seven days ago she and Kent had been in the midst of deciding to call their wedding off.

Somewhat guiltily, Bella wondered how Kent was

feeling now. She hoped he'd had a smoother week than she'd had.

A week…

Good grief. With a slam of shock, she remembered that this was Saturday. It should have been her wedding day. In fact—oh, my God—the ceremony would have been coming to a close right about now. If she and Kent hadn't changed their plans, they would be married. They'd have been in the garden at Willara Downs, surrounded by their friends and family, about to walk down the aisle. Or rather, the garden path lined with the lovely battery-operated candles that Zoe had bought to add a romantic touch.

They'd be husband and wife.

From as far back as Bella could remember, Kent had been her neighbour and her closest friend, and now she was overcome by an urge to make contact with him. To make sure he was okay.

Without a moment's hesitation, she grabbed her phone and dialled his number.

It rang and rang until she got his voice mail asking her to leave a message.

Bella wasn't in the mood to leave a message. She wanted contact. But it was pretty obvious that Kent didn't have his mobile with him, so she rang the Willara Downs number.

It also rang out then went through to voice mail and, perhaps irrationally, Bella's need to speak to Kent quadrupled. Where was he? Why wasn't he available? Was he all right?

She rang his parents.

His mother, Stephanie, answered and of course she wanted to ask all sorts of questions about Bella's trip north and about her grandfather and the cyclone. It was some time before Bella could say, 'I've been trying to get in touch with Kent.'

'Oh,' Stephanie responded warily. 'Kent's gone away for the weekend, Bella. Have you tried his mobile?'

Bella told Stephanie that she had, but as Stephanie didn't offer to tell her where Kent was she had no choice but to finish the call.

She felt more isolated and in need of a chat than ever. She decided that if she couldn't speak to Kent, she would try Zoe in Brisbane.

Zoe's response was another surprise.

'Ooh, hello, Bella. How are you?' Her friend's voice sounded different—as if she was all bubbly and keyed up and trying hard to hold the lid on her excitement. 'Did you want Kent for anything important?'

'Not really. It's just that the wedding was supposed to be happening right about now, and I guess I wanted to make sure he's okay.'

'Of course.' Zoe made sympathetic noises, but then Bella heard her asking someone, in a stage whisper, to turn the sauce down on the stove.

'Zoe, is someone with you?'

'Just—a—a friend over for dinner.'

Now there was an air of exaggerated nonchalance in Zoe's voice and Bella's curiosity skyrocketed. She had to ask. 'Would this friend be male, by any chance?'

Zoe didn't answer.

'Zoe, it's a guy, isn't it?' Bella knew Zoe hadn't had a boyfriend for ages, so this was big news. Huge.

'Yes, it's a guy. But, Bell, I'm sorry. The dinner's burning, and I've got to go. But it's been fantastic to hear from you and to know you're okay.'

'Okay. I can take a hint.' Even though her own life was a mess, Bella could smile at her friend's good fortune. 'If you do hear from Kent, tell him that I rang and I'm fine.'

'I will, and I'll tell him you were thinking of him.'

'Thanks.'

For a fanciful moment, as Bella hung up, she wondered if Zoe's guest might actually be Kent. It was rather interesting that his mysterious disappearance coincided with Zoe's mystery male guest, but she wouldn't be able to find out any more tonight.

At least the phone calls had momentarily distracted her from her own sorry situation.

But as she set the phone down on the nightstand and flopped onto her bed, the reality of her circumstances came back with a vengeance. In one short week, she'd made the mistake of falling in love with Damon Cavello. More deeply than ever.

With every conversation, with each recollection and shared smile he'd been reeling her in. Every time their gazes held for slightly longer than was strictly necessary she'd felt those strings of firecrackers lighting inside her.

Looking back on this past week, she could see that even the tense moments—their trouble with the police and the first night in the shared motel room—had been drawing them closer and relighting her hopes.

And that was before their never-to-be-forgotten night in Cardwell and all those other memories—the sheer fabulousness of total intimacy with Damon at last.

Whenever she closed her eyes, she was in heaven again, remembering the taste of his kisses and the amazing thrill of skin-to-skin contact and of having him in-side her. At last.

Oh, help. With a cry of self-pity, Bella flopped back on the bed, flinging her arms so dramatically wide that she knocked something from her nightstand and sent it flying onto the carpet.

She had no idea what it was and she almost didn't care, but after a while she rolled onto her side, glow-ered gloomily down, and saw it was a shell.

The shell Damon had found on the beach.

Sighing, she reached down and picked it up. Levering onto one elbow, she held it, running her fingers over the faint, barely-there ridges on its shiny surface.

It reminds me of you, Damon had told her in Cardwell. *It looks feminine and fragile, but it's actu-ally quite tough and brave.*

Which was hardly the truth.

Here she was totally unbrave, wanting nothing more than to be back in Damon's bed. But instead of show-ing courage, instead of doing something about it, she was hiding in her room like a coward.

Damon couldn't believe he was still pacing a motel room alone, with only his own messed-up thoughts for company, while the woman he wanted was right next door.

It was a crazy, unheard-of situation. He'd always considered himself a man of action and yet here he was, thinking about Bella, recalling everything he loved about Bella, everything he'd always loved about her, wanting her more than he'd wanted any woman and sure that he could never be at peace without her.

Yet he knew he wouldn't go to her.

Of course he *couldn't* go to her tonight. Sensibly, she'd made that clear.

Getting together for one last night was wrong on all sorts of levels. There could be nothing light-hearted about tonight. He and Bella shared too much history, too many memories. He'd promised himself he wouldn't mess with her emotions again. He couldn't behave the way he did when he was eighteen, getting in deeper and deeper and then running away.

Bella had her own plans. Her own new horizons—a new job, travel, and, somewhere out there, Mr Right, waiting in the wings.

So there was no question. He had no choice but to endure this night and then, in the morning, to get Bella safely onto the plane to Brisbane.

Unhappily resigned, Damon finally gave up pacing and began to undo his shirt buttons. With the top buttons freed, he was in the process of hauling his shirt over his head when he heard a knock at the door.

Frowning, he let the shirt fall and opened the door. His heart thudded hard. 'Bella.'

'I—ah—we forgot the coffee,' she said, shyly holding up a jar. 'I promised to make you some earlier.'

'So you did.' Damon was pleased he managed to speak calmly, given the sudden, savage pounding of his heart. 'Would you like to come in?'

'Thanks.'

He stepped back to allow her entry, and she slipped past him. Slim hipped, long legged, and as graceful as a willow. A faint hint of her wildflower perfume drifted to him. The overhead light turned her hair to shiny gold. It took every ounce of his self-restraint to refrain from hauling her into his arms.

Bella crossed straight to the kettle in the corner of his room and switched it on.

'I presume the mugs are in here?' She turned to him, eyes wide, cheeks flushed, lips softly parted. Her hair was no longer in her habitual scraped-off-her-face ponytail, but falling softly to her shoulders.

For a moment she looked uncertain and shy, but then, as if she'd made a quick decision, her expression changed. 'Actually, we could leave the coffee till later, couldn't we?'

'Later?' he repeated, his voice gruff with surprise.

With a subtle but provocative swing of her hips, she began to walk towards him. 'You weren't planning to send me away, were you, Damon?'

'But you—you—we agreed—'

She came closer, close enough to cause a hitch in his breathing and a throb in his loins. Touching close. He could smell the clean, lingering scent of shampoo in her hair.

'I know what I said, but I'm exercising my feminine right to change my mind.'

There was a sparkle in her eyes, now, the game-for-anything look of the young, seventeen-year-old Bella, the girl who'd asked him for a kiss before she'd agreed to drive to Meandarra with him.

Cheeks flushed, but with a brave little smile, she undid the next of his shirt buttons. 'I've decided that I want this, Damon. I know you're bad for me, but it's okay. You're not going to be around long enough to become a bad habit.'

Her eyes were enormous as she skimmed her fingers over his chest, sending shivers of lust arrowing low.

'I ask only one thing.' She lifted her chin, and met

his gaze bravely. 'We can't keep going on like this. If we meet up in the future, we can't start up another temporary relationship.'

Her lovely green eyes were suddenly too bright and shiny. 'This last night will have to be the end. Do you agree?'

No. He didn't want to agree to stay away from her forever.

But of course her request was reasonable.

The words *I love you* lined up in Damon's head and he imagined saying them out loud. They could make such a difference.

A lifetime of difference.

But Bella wasn't asking for a lifetime. She was playing it safe, just as he was, offering him the same terms he'd offered her a few days earlier. One night.

Wise girl. She was right. She couldn't risk having him become a bad habit. But he was walking on a razor's edge between the danger of 'I love you' and the safety of farewell sex.

The choice would be easy if he could trust himself to love and be loved in return. But how could a man as restless as the ocean offer a girl like Bella the stability and happy ever after she deserved?

Unhappily, he said at last, 'You're right. But I think—'

Bella began to trail kisses over his chest, blasting the final words of caution from his thoughts.

'You think too much,' she whispered against his lips, and then she wound her arms around his neck, pressed her parted, needy lips against his.

After that, he couldn't even remember what he'd been

going to say. All else was lost as they moved together in a lazy, lip-locked two-step dance, and Damon set about fulfilling every one of Bella's bad-boy fantasies.

CHAPTER ELEVEN

THAT night, Bella felt a kinship with lovers about to be separated by war, or impending disaster—two people sharing emotionally charged tenderness and passion before saying goodbye.

But like a song without words there was so much implied, but *too much* that they'd dared not say.

So many times she ached to tell Damon that she loved him, but she was afraid he would think she was trying to stop him from leaving.

And didn't every girl know there was no point in trying to hold on to a man who needed to be set free?

In the darkness, Damon left the bed where Bella slept and went to the window. Staring outside, he felt as dark inside as the starless night. How could anyone imagine that farewell sex was a great idea?

And yet the crazy thing was that for most of his life *goodbye* had been his favourite word. Goodbye, Willara. Goodbye, Australia. Goodbye, Dad…

Goodbyes had been his ticket of leave. Goodbyes meant freedom and moving on, shrugging off the past and starting a new chapter.

Even when it came to the women in his life, he'd always planned an escape route from the first meeting.

Not so with Bella, of course. None of this applied to Bella. Saying goodbye to her now was even more difficult than it had been in his angst-ridden teens.

Last time he'd left her, she'd begged and pleaded. This time she'd calmly seduced him.

You're not going to be around long enough to become a bad habit.

In ten years, Bella Shaw had become a wise woman, while Damon Cavello hadn't learned a damn thing.

'What time's your flight?' Damon asked as Bella handed him a steaming mug of coffee the next morning.

'Ten-thirty.'

He frowned as he glanced at the clock. 'We don't have much time, then. It's at least forty-five minutes to Cairns airport.'

Bella sighed as she picked up her mug. 'I guess I'd better take this through to my room and shower and pack.'

Damon's response was an unsmiling nod.

'See you in about twenty minutes,' she said, heading for the door.

Businesslike efficiency was the only way to get through this morning. It was too late now for heart-searching confidences, too late to tell Damon how she really felt about leaving him. This morning Bella couldn't allow herself to feel. She had to keep her thoughts focused on what lay ahead of her—the flight to Brisbane and going home to her little flat, then hunting for a new job, and talking to a travel agent, and catching up with Zoe…

She shampooed her hair, hastily painted her finger-nails emerald green, threw her clothes into her bag and was ready by the car inside twenty minutes.

Her heart stood still when Damon emerged, freshly showered, with his dark hair still damp and strangely smooth, and wearing a white T-shirt that gleamed against his dark skin. Blue jeans.

She adored everything about the way he looked. This week he'd been such good company, and he'd been so nice to Jessie and so incredibly, all-round helpful. As for the nights she'd spent with him...

How on earth was she going to find the strength to get on the plane?

The forty-five-minute journey to the airport felt ex-cruciatingly long. Bella was too aware of the smell of soap on Damon's skin. Fresh and clean with a hint of something spicy, like sandalwood or ginger. She wanted to close her eyes and to lean in to him.

Stop thinking about last night.

The journey wasn't made any easier by the fact that neither she nor Damon was in the mood for light conver-sation. Damon made one or two stiff comments about the weather, but for much of the time they sat in tense silence.

Bella stared out at the palm-tree-fringed sea, spar-kling in the tropical sun. A corner of her mind reg-istered its beauty, but mostly she was dangerously, foolishly, lost in the past. Their past.

She remembered the day they drove all the way to Meandarra. Lazy winter afternoons curled up on sofas in front of the fire in the lounge room at her parents' homestead, reading history books together, or quizzing each other before a chemistry test. Conversations about everything under the sun. Popcorn-flavoured kisses in the back of Willara's one and only movie theatre.

In this last week they'd created so many more memories, bittersweet memories that would haunt her forever.

She was grateful when they reached Cairns at last and she could pretend an interest in houses and shops and streams of traffic.

'Don't worry about coming in with me,' she told Damon when they reached the airport. 'You can just drop me off. I'll be fine.'

'Don't be silly.'

Her eyes widened, but he didn't clarify his reprimand and she didn't ask him to. Tension reigned supreme.

After parking the car, Damon insisted on carrying her bag even though it was only a small overnight bag and quite light. Bella checked in and they went through security. In the departure lounge they were surrounded by a sea of travellers—happy tourists in brightly coloured tropical clothes, happy family groups, businessmen, couples.

Couples arm in arm, couples chatting and sharing loving smiles, or couples simply sitting reading, yet still looking entirely comfortable together.

Standing with Damon near the departures display board, Bella hoped she looked as relaxed as everyone else, but it was unlikely given that she felt as tense as a guerrilla fighter stalking in a jungle. She was remembering the last time she'd said goodbye to him. When she was seventeen.

There'd been tears then. Copious tears. She'd pleaded and Damon had been stubbornly determined that she was better off without him.

Today she was determined to retain her dignity. But

when Damon touched her on the shoulder she almost jumped out of her skin.

'Hey, I didn't mean to startle you.'

She let out her breath with a soft huff. 'Sorry. I've never been great at goodbyes.' She swallowed the enormous lump in her throat. 'What do you say at a time like this? It's been nice to catch up with you again?'

His mouth tilted in a smile that came nowhere near his eyes. 'It's the truth, *bellissima*. It's been fabulous to catch up with you again.'

He reached for her hands and looked down at them as he rubbed the pads of his thumbs over the emerald nail polish. 'Every morning I'm going to wake up and wonder what colour they are.'

'Don't say things like that.' Tears stung her eyes and she snatched her hands out of his grasp. 'No nostalgia, Damon. It's not fair.'

She saw an answering quicksilver flash in his eyes. Saw the rapid movement of his throat as he swallowed.

'And stop looking so sad,' she ordered him, sounding a thousand times tougher than she felt. 'I need you to be cool. I need you to not care.'

'That's not possible.'

Bella might have burst into tears if there hadn't been a sudden blaring announcement that her flight was boarding.

She pasted on a stiff little smile as the passengers for her flight began to line up. She took her boarding pass out of her bag, hitched the bag over her shoulder. Any minute now, her bravado would collapse. She had to hold herself together for just a little longer.

'Where are you off to next?' she asked Damon, needing to talk about anything except goodbye.

He shrugged. 'Looks like it might be Hong Kong.'

'That should be nice. I hope you get lots of great stories.' She would probably see him on TV, sauntering past stalls in a crowded market in Kowloon, or interviewing a high-profile Chinese businessman.

She set her gaze at middle distance, not daring to catch his eye. 'I'd better be going.'

'Yeah.' He released the word on a sigh.

Quickly she kissed his cheek, then stepped back, out of harm's way. 'Thanks for taking care of Paddy and Violet.'

'My pleasure.'

'I hope you have a safe journey.'

'You, too, Bella.'

The line of passengers was moving quickly and there was absolutely no point in prolonging this agony.

'I'll be off, then.' She turned quickly so he couldn't see her tears.

Without looking back, she joined the line of passengers having their boarding passes checked. She thought, if this was a movie, Damon would come running after her now, and he'd tell her he loved her and he'd beg her to stay, and she'd happily run away with him and be with him forever.

It didn't happen, of course. Already she was entering the tunnel that led to the plane, and she didn't look back, couldn't bear to see him still standing in the same spot, or worse, already walking away.

'Welcome aboard,' said the friendly stewardess and Bella was proud that she managed to return her smile.

'This has been quite an adventure,' Violet said as she sat beside Damon, looking out to sea.

They were staying overnight at Sarina, a tiny beach-side town about halfway down the Queensland coast. Paddy was taking an afternoon nap, but Violet had opted to join Damon on the beach.

'A little sea air will blow the cobwebs away,' she'd told him, but she'd needed his help to lower her aging bones onto the beach towel that he'd spread on the sand.

'Are you sure you're comfortable?'

'I'm fine now I'm down.' Violet laughed. 'But you'll have to help me up again.'

Dressed in slim Capri pants and a loose cotton shirt, she looked like an elderly, but still beautiful film star as she sat on the sand with her elegant hands linked around her knees. Her arms were thin and brown and blotched with age spots, but girlish clusters of silver bracelets twinkled at her fragile wrists.

Her long hair, white as a seagull's breast, had been loosened from its knot by the wind, and wispy strands blew about her face. She didn't seem to care. At eighty-three, she was having an adventure...

'I hope you're not planning to run away again,' Damon told her fondly. 'When I get you back to Willara, I expect you to stay put.'

'Oh, you mustn't worry, darling. I promise to be good.' She sent him a knowing wink. 'Or would you like another excuse for a road trip with Bella?'

Damon hastily switched his gaze to the distant horizon, but he couldn't avoid a hollow feeling of emptiness at the mention of Bella's name. 'I wouldn't inflict another trip like that on her.'

'Damon, she enjoyed it as much as you did.'

'How would you know?'

'I've known you both for a very long time. Besides, I still have my eyesight, my dear.'

He scowled at her. 'And what do you think you saw?'

'Two people very much in love.'

Dismayed, Damon stared at his grandmother. 'Now you're getting carried away.'

Violet shook her head. 'I'm not being fanciful, although I will admit I'm poking my bib in where it's probably not wanted. But someone needs to wake you up. If I had enough strength I'd seriously consider shaking some sense into you.'

'Why? What have I done that's so wrong?'

'You're planning to run away. Again.'

'Excuse me? *I'm* running away? Have you forgotten why we're here?'

'You know what I'm talking about. You're running away from Bella. And that's ridiculous, because you're thoroughly miserable. I'm sure Bella's quite wretched, too. Poor girl.'

Damon's breath came in painful gasps. He was reliving the farewell at the airport, watching Bella disappear without a backward glance. He'd never felt so suddenly, painfully empty, as if he'd been drained of something vital, like his blood.

'Darling,' Violet said gently. 'You have so much to offer a young woman.'

'Now that's where you're wrong. A girl with any sense would not want to tie herself to someone who deals with danger on a daily basis.'

'Oh, for heaven's sake. Do you really think a little danger would worry Bella?'

With a growl of frustration, Damon jumped to his feet, dragged in great gulps of sharp, salty air. But almost immediately he felt foolish, and when he turned back to his grandmother she looked so diminutive and helpless alone on the sand that he quickly dropped down beside her again and let out a heavy sigh.

He knew what she'd said was true. Bella had never been a girl to be frightened of a little daring and danger. If he didn't already know it, she'd told him as much several times.

After what felt like an age, he said, 'Do you want to know the truth?'

'If you're ready to tell me.'

'If I'm *ready?*' He stared at her. Stared at the dearly loved, wrinkled face and the bright, dark, knowing eyes he knew so well. 'Are you implying that you already know what I'm going to tell you?'

'You said it was the truth.'

'Well, yes. That's right.'

'The truth that lies in your heart?'

His heart thudded heavily. 'Yes.'

Violet's smile was warm. 'I've been waiting to hear this for a very long time.'

'You think I love Bella?'

His grandmother nodded slowly. 'I know you do, Damon.'

He felt despair rising through him like a tide, squeezing the air from his lungs. 'If that's true, why can't I tell her?'

'Because you're prepared to take risks with your body on a daily basis, but you won't take a risk with your heart.'

'Why?'

It felt like the most important question he'd ever asked, and it was some time before Violet answered.

Eventually, she said, 'I suspect you're worried you'll end up abandoned like your father.'

It was true. Of course. It was suddenly blindingly true. On some level he must have always known this, but he'd never allowed his thoughts to linger on this truth. He'd always snatched them away, as if they could burn him.

'Damon, you know it's hogwash.' Violet's wrinkled hand gripped his arm. 'You're nothing like your father. You never have been and you never will be.'

He let out the breath he hadn't realised he'd been holding. 'Thanks,' he said quietly. 'I think I needed to hear that from you.'

Ahead of him the blue-green sea swelled and splashed in white-capped peaks. Streaks of pink, a reflection of the sunset behind them, were spreading across the sky. The world looked suddenly, wonderfully brighter.

Bella checked her appearance in the mirror one last time. Her hair was pulled back into a tidy bun, her make-up was flattering, but subdued. Her outfit was a grey pencil skirt with a matching grey-and-white striped blouse, modestly buttoned high. She was pleased with the result. She looked suitably conservative from top to toe. Even her fingernails were an unadventurous pale pink.

So...she was ready for her job interview and, if she was really lucky, by the time she arrived home this afternoon she would be once again employed.

It had been a stroke of good fortune discovering the online advertisement for a 'motivated personal assistant.' The job was right up her alley, and she'd been able to email a cover letter and résumé mere moments before the applications closed.

More importantly, the mad dash to get her documentation in order had helped to distract her from the pain of her heart breaking into a thousand bleeding pieces—a condition she'd endured from the moment she'd stepped onto the plane in Cairns.

Regret was such a useless emotion. Bella knew that, but she'd been swamped by an ocean of remorse. She was so mad with herself for walking away without admitting that she loved Damon, that she didn't care how dangerous his work was, or how remote, she wanted and needed and longed to be with him.

He might not have been pleased to hear this news. Then again, if she'd explained that she didn't expect him to come back to a safe office job in Australia, he might have been secretly delighted.

Now she would never know.

She'd walked away from the only man she'd ever loved, and now she was suffering the awful consequences.

To distract herself, she'd dived straight into hunting for work, and this morning she'd actually been able to stop thinking about Damon for at least ten minutes. Once she started work, she hoped to stretch those Damon-free minutes into hours, and eventually into days and weeks.

Getting this job was important. Her sanity saver. But she'd spent too long getting ready. She was running out of time and in danger of missing her bus…

All she needed was to find her grey handbag and her bus ticket…and her references…

Bella had just found the last of these items when her

front doorbell rang. *Panic.* She had no idea who the caller could be. Her friends were all at work.

A hasty glance down the hallway to the frosted-glass panel in her front door revealed a tall, dark, masculine outline. *No.* The last thing she wanted now was to be delayed by a talkative, foot-in-the-door salesman.

She was hopeless with salespeople. She found it almost impossible to shut the door in their faces. It seemed too rude. So she always found herself listening to their spiel and then taking an age to get rid of them.

If she was held up now, she'd miss her bus and be late for her interview.

She decided to sneak out the back way. It was a bit of a nuisance, ducking lines of washing and children's tricycles, but with luck the fellow would be gone by the time she got round to the front of her block of flats.

Damon pressed the front door bell again, and his stomach tied itself into a dozen knots as its ringing reverberated through Bella's flat.

It was clear she wasn't home, and, of course, he'd known it wasn't wise to race down to Brisbane without phoning ahead. But he'd been impatient. And, yeah, afraid that Bella would simply tell him to get lost without giving him a chance to explain.

This morning, after a final quick check to make sure that Paddy and Violet were happily resettled in Greenacres, he'd headed straight down the Toowoomba Range to the city, with a heart full of hope, planning to catch Bella before she went out.

Obviously, he was too late.

He made his way back down the steps feeling more depressed than he would have believed. On the footpath, he stood, staring at Bella's letterbox, debating whether it was worth leaving a note.

But too much depended on getting this meeting right. *Everything* depended on getting it right. And Damon wanted to be face to face with Bella when he told her all that he needed to say.

Disappointed, he turned back to his car. Two doors away a bus was pulling into a stop and a slim blonde girl in a grey skirt and high heels climbed into it.

A gong struck inside Damon. Surely that girl was Bella? How could he have missed seeing her?

He began to run, and as the bus pulled away from the kerb he saw Bella sitting in a window seat, staring straight ahead. He waved madly.

'Bella,' he shouted, waving both arms above his head, trying to catch her eye.

The bus accelerated, zipping her away down the street. Out of sight.

Again.

Bella arrived at the job interview with only minutes to spare, but at least she had a chance to catch her breath and to compose herself. She dredged up a smile as she introduced herself at the front desk and was shown to a room where two other girls sat on chairs lined up against the wall.

They eyed her warily when she walked in. She smiled. 'Hi.'

They returned her smile half-heartedly.

Bella took a seat, drew a deep breath and tried to feel calm and serene. And confident. Confidence went a long way in a job interview.

She tried a little visualisation technique she'd learned

during one of the many vocational training days she'd attended. She imagined being told she had won this job, pictured shaking her new boss's hand. Heard him ask, 'Can you start next Monday?'

'Sure,' she'd say. 'That would be wonderful.'

Except…it wouldn't be wonderful.

She'd be telling a lie.

How could starting a new job be wonderful when all she really wanted was to be with Damon?

She closed her eyes and drew a shuddering breath.

'I'm nervous, too,' the girl next to her whispered.

Bella's eyes flashed open. 'I'm not really nervous,' she said. 'Not about the job.'

'You're lucky. I probably shouldn't care so much, but it's my dream to get a job like this.'

'Well, yes. It does sound good.' Somewhat guiltily, Bella eyed the earnest expression on the other girl's face.

Just then, a door opened and another applicant came out. She flashed them an eyebrow-raised smile of relief.

'Miranda Hoey,' boomed a masculine voice and the girl near the door jumped to her feet and smoothed down her skirt.

As Bella watched the door close behind her she felt cold all over, and her stomach churned uncomfortably. The air in the room seemed to solidify. She couldn't breathe.

'Excuse me,' she whispered to her neighbour and she lurched to her feet.

At the front desk, she said, 'I'm sorry. I've changed my mind. I'd like to withdraw my application.'

Outside on the city street, she drew in several deep breaths and felt marginally better.

'I have no idea why I did that,' she said to no one in particular. But she smiled. And for no reason that made any sense, she felt marvellously free.

It was late afternoon by the time Bella got back to her flat. She'd splurged on lunch in the city at a favourite café, and she'd gone clothes shopping. Lingerie shopping to be precise, which was rather reckless given that she didn't have a job and she was still paying off a wedding dress that she would never wear.

She'd been thinking about Damon far too often as she'd shopped. She'd wondered if he'd already left for Hong Kong, and she'd even played with the ridiculous fantasy of jumping on a plane and following him—just to see how he'd react.

Okay, so she'd told him she didn't want to continue their relationship. But might things be different if she told him her true feelings? What did she have to lose? She couldn't be any more miserable than she was now.

She was rather tired by the time she climbed from the bus, lugging her shopping, including a ready-made chicken satay that she would heat in the microwave and eat in front of the telly.

She didn't see the man getting out of the car in front of her flat until he almost blocked her path.

She got such a shock, her shopping bags slipped from her suddenly nerveless fingers. 'Damon!'

Damon, looking all kinds of wonderful. Damon, stooping to gather up the packet of chicken satay and the silk and lace undies.

What was he doing here? She'd told him to stay away. She should be angry.

'I—I wasn't expecting you,' she spluttered.

'I've been waiting here since this morning.'

'This morning?' Bella tried to swallow a sudden lump in her throat. 'Why?'

Cautiously, he said, 'I needed to see you, but you were too busy hopping on to a bus and getting away. I hoped you wouldn't be gone too long.'

Her jaw dropped. Her heart was performing somersaults at the very thought of impatient, restless Damon waiting here. All day.

She shook her head in stunned disbelief. 'I thought you were a salesman. I only saw a shadow through the front door and I was in a hurry. I didn't want to be late. I'm sorry, Damon. I can't believe you've been waiting all this time.'

They were standing on the footpath in full view of her neighbours. 'You'd better come inside,' she said.

Damon smiled. 'I thought you'd never ask.'

An entire flock of butterflies danced in Bella's stomach as he followed her up her front stairs, carrying her shopping. She wasn't sure if she should be happy and excited, or scared and angry.

'I think I left the place in a bit of a mess,' she said as she pushed the door open. 'I was rushing around this morning getting ready for a job interview. The kitchen's through here.'

She led the way to the tiny kitchen at the back of her flat. 'I'll need to get that chicken in the fridge.' She had no idea why she was babbling about kitchens and chickens. She supposed it was nerves.

'Would you like some coffee?' she called over her shoulder. 'You must be parched.'

'I've had three cups of takeaway coffee.'

'Oh. I guess you don't need any more caffeine, then.'

'You said you've been for a job interview?'

Turning, Bella saw surprising bleak shadows in Damon's eyes. Her heart became a bird dashing its wings against the cage of her chest.

He was pale and frowning as he set the shopping bags on the kitchen table. 'Did you get the job?'

Bella hesitated. When she'd walked away from the interview this morning, this man had been at the forefront of her mind. But if she admitted how she felt about him now, she would feel so vulnerable...

She still didn't know why he was here. Why had he waited for her? Why should he care if she'd applied for a new job?

It was clear, however, as Damon stood to attention, waiting for her answer, that he *did* care.

'I changed my mind,' she said quietly. 'I pulled out of the interview.'

'Why?'

'I wasn't absolutely sure it was what I wanted. If I'd been offered the position, I might have felt...trapped.'

She watched the slow roll of his broad shoulders as he relaxed, saw the almost imperceptible dawning of a smile.

Afternoon sunlight streamed softly through the only window in the room highlighting the rumpled sheen of his hair and the jut of his cheekbones. She thought he'd never looked more masculine and handsome than he did right now.

Bravely, she said, 'Now it's your turn, Damon. You need to explain what you're doing here when we agreed it's all over between us.' She felt as if she were poised at the top of a very high peak, and she knew, instinctively, that Damon was about to lift her to the heights of happiness, or tip her into the pits of despair.

'I have a confession to make,' he said.

Bella drew a deep, very necessary breath.

Damon looked tense, too. Gripping the back of a kitchen chair with both hands, he said, 'I'm here to tell you something I've been too scared to admit.'

'What's that?'

'I love you.' His eyes took on a bright silver sheen and his throat rippled as he gripped the chair harder. 'I've never told you before, Bella, because I couldn't risk having you turn me down. But now I know I no longer have a choice. I love you so much. I *need* you so much, and I know I'm a bad risk—but I—'

She didn't give him a chance to continue. With a whoop of delight she dived across the room and was in his arms.

'You're an idiot,' she told him as she kissed him.

'I know.'

'But I'm an idiot, too. I was trying to tell you in Cairns that I love you. That I've never stopped loving you, and you've totally ruined me for anyone else. But I was scared, too.'

'Oh, Bella.' His arms tightened around her.

'I was scared because I always knew you needed to stay free.'

'We have to talk about that.'

'But it doesn't matter now. Not if we both love each other. We'll work something out.'

With a soft groan, he pulled her in and kissed her with everything that lay in his heart.

Later, they talked. On the sofa in the front room. With Bella nestled between his legs and the lights

turned low. Damon knew he'd never felt more contented.

'About my job,' he said.

Bella rubbed her cheek against his jaw. 'Please don't
start making sacrifices. I don't expect you to come
home and settle down. I don't think I'd enjoy having
the wanderer captive at last.'

'Would you be prepared to live somewhere abroad,
then, like—say—Hong Kong?'

'Damon, I'd love it.'

He chuckled. 'You always were an adventurer. But
I'd still be away for weeks at a time.'

'That's okay. I'll cope. I'd quite enjoy exploring Hong
Kong on my own.'

'What about your father? Will he be all right without you?'

'He's being very good now. Following doctor's orders to the letter. And Kent will keep an eye on him.'

'You could fly back whenever you wanted to.'

Damon slipped his arms around Bella's waist and
held her more tightly. 'And I won't stay in the same job
forever. There's this guy I know—a foreign correspondent who works in Toronto. He flies overseas to cover
special stories, and he consults his wife and daughters
before he takes on a job.'

'Wow. Does his family really have a say?'

'Sure. The girls wouldn't let him go on a job where
there'd been particularly nasty suicide bombings. When
he was given the case, they looked it up on the internet.
They asked their dad how he would know if someone
had a bomb under his shirt.'

'Good question. How would he know?'

'He wouldn't. So the girls said he shouldn't take the job.'

'Clever girls.' Bella sat up and turned to him. 'But why are you telling me this? You're not planning on having daughters.'

Damon smiled. 'Not until after we're married.'

Her eyes widened with surprise. 'I don't believe you said that.'

Still smiling, Damon drew a ring from his pocket. 'Would you believe me now?'

Now there were tears in Bella's eyes as she stared at the diamond-and-ruby engagement ring.

She touched the ring with her fingertip. 'It's so beautiful. I know this sounds strange, but it seems familiar.'

'It was Violet's engagement ring. I told her I was coming to Brisbane to see you and she guessed. She wanted you to have it.'

'Oh, Damon. How gorgeous. How sweet of her.'

The tears streamed down Bella's face as he slipped the ring onto her finger. She dashed at them with the heel of her hand and tried to smile. 'I'm glad I'm wearing pale pink nail polish today. I'd hate to spoil this elegant ring with something too out there.'

'Don't tell me your fingernails will be boring from now on.'

She rubbed her bare foot against his. 'I can still be as daring as I like with my toenails.' Another tear fell and she swiped at it. 'I'm not sad. Honestly. These are tears of happiness.'

Damon was happy, too. In fact, he couldn't believe how happy and calm he was. He'd expected to feel terrified at the prospect of pledging himself to one woman for the rest of his life, but as he drew his fiancée into his arms he was aware of the ten lonely years he'd spent without her, and he felt nothing but certainty and astonishing joy.

EPILOGUE

It was a crisp, pale winter's evening when Bella and Damon arrived at Willara Downs. Although it wasn't quite dark, the lights were on in the homestead and as they drove up to the front steps they could see smoke curling from the chimney.

A door swung open spilling yellow light down the steps and into the garden. Kent and Zoe's one-year-old son, Harry, came toddling ahead of his father, arms wide in welcome.

Bella was laughing as she jumped out of the car and hugged little Harry and then Kent.

'It's wonderful to be home,' she said, looking about her, beyond the homestead gardens to the paddocks lush after a good wet season.

'Did you see Blue Gums as you drove past?' Kent asked.

Bella nodded. 'It was weird to know strangers are living there now, but I hear they're very good tenants.'

A year ago, her father had finally moved off the Blue Gums farm and was now living in a cottage in town. He was a regular visitor at Greenacres and he was bringing Paddy and Violet to join in this evening's festivities.

They were celebrating a mock Christmas in July,

which was Zoe's idea. 'You always seem to be away at Christmas time, and it's too hot anyway. In July we can have traditional roast turkey and plum pudding in front of the fire.'

'Sounds perfect,' Bella and Damon agreed.

Bella smiled as Damon joined her, throwing an arm around her shoulders. They'd been based in Hong Kong for four years and they'd been the happiest years of her life. Apart from sharing Damon's life, a joy which couldn't be overestimated, she loved the lifestyle.

She loved exploring the crowded market places and the fascinating narrow streets, or catching the Star Ferry to discover the outer islands. She enjoyed getting to know the other journalists' wives over noisy, laughter-filled lunches. She'd studied Chinese calligraphy and discovered a whole new art form.

But it was good to be home. Bella hadn't realised till now just how uplifting it was to revisit familiar places and people.

While Kent took Damon to the back veranda to fetch a beer from the second fridge, Bella found Zoe in the kitchen.

'How's my favourite farmer's wife?' She was grinning broadly as she gave her best friend a hug, and remembered once again how overjoyed she was when Zoe and Kent announced their engagement after returning from—of all places—Prague.

She knew Zoe would relish her role as a farmer's wife, and indeed Zoe threw herself into the lifestyle with gusto. She grew parsley and shallots and rhubarb for the farmers' markets and she was always making relishes and jams and preserves.

This evening Zoe's kitchen was filled with delicious

roasting smells. She was glowing with good health and happiness.

'Let me look at you,' Zoe said now, releasing Bella from a bear hug and holding her at arm's length. 'You look fabulous.' Her eyes narrowed as she stared hard at Bella. 'And do I detect a glow?'

Bella blushed.

Zoe squealed. Then dropped her voice to a whisper. 'Am I right? Is there a baby on the way?'

'I wasn't going to say anything, yet. I haven't told Dad or Paddy.'

Zoe shrieked and hugged Bella again. 'I won't say a word, but I'm so excited. I'm going to be an aunty.'

'Well, sort of.' Bella laughed. 'Even though we're not related.'

'Well, a godmother, then. Or something.'

'You'll certainly be a VIP in our baby's life. I like the sound of Aunty Zoe.'

'Is Damon pleased?'

'Pleased? He can't stop grinning. By the way, there's one other bit of news.'

'Not twins?'

Bella rolled her eyes. 'Heavens, no. At least I don't think so. But we're relocating to Brisbane.'

'Oh, Bella. That's wonderful. You must be so happy.'

'We're both ready to come home.' She didn't mention that Damon had made a 'kind of' truce with his dad, who also lived in Brisbane. Instead she patted her tummy. 'We want this little guy to grow up in Oz.' As Bella said this she looked around, then asked, 'Where's Abbey?'

Abbey was Zoe and Kent's three-year-old daughter, as adorable as she was mischievous.

'That's a good question,' said Zoe. 'Where *is* Abbey? I take it she wasn't with Kent to welcome you?'

'No. I only saw Harry.'

Zoe frowned. 'I hope she's not rearranging my table decorations.'

Behind her, the oven pinged.

'Would you like me to check the dining room?' Bella asked.

'Thanks. I need to baste this turkey.'

In the dining room, Bella discovered a long white table covered in crisp white cloths and gleaming silver, with wine glasses shining like bubbles. There were tasteful centrepieces made with pine cones and ivy. Everything looked in place.

She heard a sound coming from the lounge room next door, and poked her head around the doorway.

She gasped when she saw Abbey sitting in front of the fire with a hen in her lap. There were two more hens in a doll's pram. A fourth was scratching at the carpet.

Abbey turned and she saw Bella and put a finger to her lips. 'Shh,' she whispered. 'The chooks is going to sleep.'

Bella clapped a hand over her mouth to hold back her laughter. She tiptoed forward. 'Does Mummy know you have the chickens in here?'

Abbey shook her head. 'No, I'll get into trouble. But I had to bring them into the fire, Bella. It's too cold outside.'

Bella smiled and suggested that the adults would be coming in here soon, including Abbey's grandparents. 'Mummy might be cross, so I think we should put the chooks back in the hen house with plenty of straw to keep them warm,' she said. 'Wait here a minute while I get Damon to help me smuggle them out.'

Five minutes later, Bella and Damon were running back across the yard from the hen house, their secret mission accomplished. Their breath made white smoke in the frosty air. On the back veranda they paused before going back into the warm house.

'Come here,' Damon said, drawing Bella into his arms and nuzzling her cheek. 'Have I told you you're the prettiest mother-to-be in Australia?'

'Once or twice,' she said, hugging him.

'Do you think our little one will get up to tricks like Abbey?'

Bella smiled and kissed the tip of his cold nose. 'With you as his father I think there's every chance he'll be a gorgeous little bad boy.'

'Or girl.'

Laughing, they went, arm in arm, inside.

* * * * *

ROMANCE

HISTORICAL

MEDICAL

Mills & Boon® Large Print

January 2012

ROMANCE

The Kanellis Scandal	Michelle Reid
Monarch of the Sands	Sharon Kendrick
One Night in the Orient	Robyn Donald
His Poor Little Rich Girl	Melanie Milburne
From Daredevil to Devoted Daddy	Barbara McMahon
Little Cowgirl Needs a Mum	Patricia Thayer
To Wed a Rancher	Myrna Mackenzie
The Secret Princess	Jessica Hart

HISTORICAL

Seduced by the Scoundrel	Louise Allen
Unmasking the Duke's Mistress	Margaret McPhee
To Catch a Husband...	Sarah Mallory
The Highlander's Redemption	Marguerite Kaye

MEDICAL

The Playboy of Harley Street	Anne Fraser
Doctor on the Red Carpet	Anne Fraser
Just One Last Night...	Amy Andrews
Suddenly Single Sophie	Leonie Knight
The Doctor & the Runaway Heiress	Marion Lennox
The Surgeon She Never Forgot	Melanie Milburne

1211 GEN STD LP

Mills & Boon® Hardback

February 2012

ROMANCE

An Offer She Can't Refuse	Emma Darcy
An Indecent Proposition	Carol Marinelli
A Night of Living Dangerously	Jennie Lucas
A Devilishly Dark Deal	Maggie Cox
Marriage Behind the Façade	Lynn Raye Harris
Forbidden to His Touch	Natasha Tate
Back in the Lion's Den	Elizabeth Power
Running From the Storm	Lee Wilkinson
Innocent 'til Proven Otherwise	Amy Andrews
Dancing with Danger	Fiona Harper
The Cop, the Puppy and Me	Cara Colter
Back in the Soldier's Arms	Soraya Lane
Invitation to the Prince's Palace	Jennie Adams
Miss Prim and the Billionaire	Lucy Gordon
The Shameless Life of Ruiz Acosta	Susan Stephens
Who Wants To Marry a Millionaire?	Nicola Marsh
Sydney Harbour Hospital: Lily's Scandal	Marion Lennox
Sydney Harbour Hospital: Zoe's Baby	Alison Roberts

HISTORICAL

The Scandalous Lord Lanchester	Anne Herries
His Compromised Countess	Deborah Hale
Destitute On His Doorstep	Helen Dickson
The Dragon and the Pearl	Jeannie Lin

MEDICAL

Gina's Little Secret	Jennifer Taylor
Taming the Lone Doc's Heart	Lucy Clark
The Runaway Nurse	Dianne Drake
The Baby Who Saved Dr Cynical	Connie Cox

Mills & Boon® Large Print

February 2012

ROMANCE

The Most Coveted Prize	Penny Jordan
The Costarella Conquest	Emma Darcy
The Night that Changed Everything	Anne McAllister
Craving the Forbidden	India Grey
Her Italian Soldier	Rebecca Winters
The Lonesome Rancher	Patricia Thayer
Nikki and the Lone Wolf	Marion Lennox
Mardie and the City Surgeon	Marion Lennox

HISTORICAL

Married to a Stranger	Louise Allen
A Dark and Brooding Gentleman	Margaret McPhee
Seducing Miss Lockwood	Helen Dickson
The Highlander's Return	Marguerite Kaye

MEDICAL

The Doctor's Reason to Stay	Dianne Drake
Career Girl in the Country	Fiona Lowe
Wedding on the Baby Ward	Lucy Clark
Special Care Baby Miracle	Lucy Clark
The Tortured Rebel	Alison Roberts
Dating Dr Delicious	Laura Iding

12 GEN STD LP